Casper Luna is a writer and poet living in Eastern North Carolina. A fan of short stories and scary fiction, he entices the reader to enter a new world of the mad and macabre, with every story they read. Filling his stories with ghosts, spooks, demons, magic, and madness, he creates worlds of insanity and fear, and places them inside of the reader.

Casper Luna

THE TOMBSTONE CONFESSIONS

AUSTIN MACAULEY PUBLISHERS™

LONDON • CAMBRIDGE • NEW YORK • SHARJAH

Ordering Information:
Quantity sales: special discounts are available on quantity purchases by corporations, associations, and others. For details, contact the publisher at the address below.

Publisher's Cataloging-in-Publication data
Luna, Casper
The Tombstone Confessions

ISBN 9781641827911 (Paperback)
ISBN 9781641827928 (Hardback)
ISBN 9781645366119 (ePub e-book)

Library of Congress Control Number: 2019939365

The main category of the book — Fiction / Horror

www.austinmacauley.com/us

First Published (2019)
Austin Macauley Publishers LLC
40 Wall Street, 28th Floor
New York, NY 10005
USA

mail-usa@austinmacauley.com
+1 (646) 5125767

To all of the friends and family who have supported me along the way, thank you.

"Hello?"

The stranger's voice just echoed out, sounding hollow and distant.

"Hello?" Again, a cry, and again silence.

"Are you ready?"

The stranger stood momentarily petrified, slowly turning his head to see a musty cemetery; something that looked out of place for his home and time. It was almost gothic to its appearance with overgrown bushes and infested with ivy and Spanish moss, looking not unlike some lost relic hidden within a swamp, forgotten to the elements and decay of time. A truly grotesque and ill-feeling sight to behold. He felt as if he were lost in some dark novel, trapped within its pages and without an escape in sight. As the man stood in confusion and wonderment at the place and situation that he now found himself in, he again heard the voice speak…

"Are you ready?"

"Am I ready? Ready for what?"

He whipped his head around, scanning the trees and bushes and tombstones upon the graves. Looking for a sign of someone, something, anything.

"Hello? Is someone there?"

Still finding nothing to confirm his efforts, only the silence of the graveyard and the calm breeze around him.

The stranger tried to peer through the darkness to see who it was that was talking to him…such a horrible voice, no life in it at all. Just a droning and waning tone that punches itself easily into your ear, and swiftly burrows in to your center. But all that he could see was the cemetery before him: headstones, crosses, decaying flowers, statues, and centered by them was a sinister yet alluring mausoleum, looking eerily reminiscent of some Victorian Estate, left to slowly rot and wither with time. And there, perched upon a cross of marble and ivory, was a grotesque-looking shadowy angel, vigilantly guarding some great resting place.

The stranger found himself standing within the heart of some graveyard, speaking not only to himself in curiosity, but it would now seem to him, he was now speaking to nothing, only shadows. The air felt musty to him, almost as if he were back home near the swamps. That thick, pungent, damp, sticky almost even, type of feel that you get when you live near the Deep South and its rivers. But for as much as he knew, he could feel the air around him, it simply felt like it was washing past him, not even making contact with him.

He felt displaced, almost as if he were in some horrid dream that he could not escape from, yet he knew that this was no dream. He knew that this was real, he knew where he was, what he was looking at…he just didn't know why he was there, what was going on, or how he even came to be there. All he could do was to try and find some way out of his present situation, to find some exit to the graveyard, or find a person or a building. To find something to let him know that this was all just some wild and crazy adventure to add to his memoirs, rather than some terrifying and unknown situation that filled him with more dread, more doubt, more pain, and more confusion and intrigue than anything he had ever known or experienced before.

As he walked down the naturally maintained path that weaved through the small woods around one corner of the cemetery, he managed to stumble across a tombstone that caught his eye. It was alone, neglected for decades, left to the terms of Mother Nature as to when it shall be retaken by the land. It was overgrown with small ivies and moss along its base. The lettering was old, it was cheaply made but not done hastily. It was scarce of anything that you would expect to be on a tombstone. It simply stated the person's name and the years that they lived, nothing else could be seen, no statements or family endearments. It seemed more like something that was mass-produced, it had a certain style and rhythm to its layout and information. No care was put into this, no love from a family member or close friend, this was given to people who didn't have any other people in their lives. People who were left to the wills and wishes of some institution, state or society, to be disposed off as cheaply and conveniently as possible. And there it sat, nestled back into its own bushy garden, left to itself and to its environment.

The stranger walked up to the gravestone and tried to read the name: Sarah Thatch.

And as her name came out across his lips, he began to see flashes; pictures in his head nearly like a memory, but so much more vivid, as if he personally had witnessed these events. He could begin to see her life, places, and situations, people, and things, all things that she remembered about her life, and held dear. He was seeing memories of the long dead woman who now lay before his feet. He could begin to hear voices from all directions around him, all speaking over each other, phasing in and out of each other as if they were all in some sickening harmony. He could hear their voices speaking to him, telling their stories, repeating the same lives over and over again, each rendition as detailed as the last. As he stood there and listened to her voice, his thoughts began to fade, and he began to see, as if her voice were narrating to him some epic tome. He began to see her, to hear her, to see memories of her life, and to experience it all through her eyes, through her flesh.

Sarah Thatch
1648–1671

Marshfield, Massachusetts

"When you make a deal with a demon, you must always pay a price. There is no 'selling your soul to the devil'…there is no devil, or at least he doesn't seem to show himself much these days. No Hell either, at least not in the sense that most think of it, with fire and rivers of lava. Just black, perfectly dark, calm, oblivion. It shifts and changes like the wind, morphing from one scene to the next almost flawlessly. There the demons hold the power; anything that you want, you can have, for the right price. You can receive long life, if you are willing to give life in exchange. You can be granted eternal beauty for the price of having to live in exile with nobody to see you, and no glass to reflect."

The fire flows around her like a current, it never touches her, gliding like liquid pain over her skin. "Never ending, never ceasing pain, damned for all time, condemned to suffer for all that I have done within their world. Here, all are punished, for all are guilty. Some are weighed after a time and are given the chance to try again, others are consigned to their fates."

The flashes became stronger, more vivid and detailed, as the events surrounding her final memories began to unfold before him.

"I have had two apprentices during the course of my faith. Both were eager, both promising in their own ways, and excelled at their respective disciplines. Both brave and honorable, and both of them failures, lost forever to abuse of magic and the ignorance regarding the consequences of that action. My first apprentice over estimated his own abilities, his will was not focused, and he was not prepared. As a result of those mistakes, he chose to end his own life after journeying to the Ethers; that is a place where you must be focused, you must be precise, and you must have the will to complete your journey; once a journey has begun, it must be seen through to the end, or you risk very real and very serious damage to not only yourself, but to others as well. He failed."

The sounds and images of watching this man climb into the rafters of his barn, followed swiftly with a short drop and a sudden stop at the end of a rope, was starting to engrave themselves into his mind. It was then that he realized that she had witnessed this death; watching him, standing below him as he swung back and forth, until the last breath in his body left him.

"My second apprentice did far better. She had a very strong will and a focus to see any task through that was placed before her. Eager, trusting, confident...her fault was vanity. She had learned of a way to achieve great wealth, great beauty, and great influence, and felt that she was strong enough to do what was required for this power. For everything that can be achieved and gained, something in turn must be surrendered and destroyed. To manipulate the actions and efforts of the world takes great power, and the price that must be paid to attain it is just as great. She could not handle the price that she had to pay: a life's debt, and in turn ran herself through with a dagger only one month after receiving her new gift."

He could hear her tears as they fell to the dirt below, and could smell her blood on the dagger as she twisted it before pulling it out of her stomach...only to thrust it back in again. He stood there, watching through the witch's eyes, as this girl, this child, began to perform seppuku upon herself, finally repaying her life debt to her demon master.

"To sustain the will to see through anything that might find its way to you and influence the course of your path is a feat that very few hold. It takes a great deal of knowledge and skill to control magical things; I remember failing before I could learn to control and focus my will, ensuring that it worked for me rather than against. But in the course of learning these rules and limitations, I paid many prices for my actions, I just simply learned how to control it."

The stranger opened his eyes, to no longer see the puritan village and this ancient and contorted woman that he had been listening to, but rather to the graveyard and tombstone that he had once looked down on. As he looked at the moss and the stone, he could still smell the blood, hear the tears, and feel the snap of the rope.

"Someday I shall have a new apprentice, I can feel a change coming, and it is coming soon."

"Now that is interesting... How often do you come across a headstone of a woman, accused, tried, and executed on suspicions of being a witch? And more than that, to find out that she was a witch! I can't imagine that turned out to be the case in every 'witch hunt' that has happened throughout the centuries, so this happens to be a unique and interesting moment for you. Today you have learned something new, imagine what you will learn tomorrow?"

Again, the man found himself pulled back to his reality, looking around for that voice.

"Who are you? What is this?"

But there was no answer. Again, the stranger found himself yelling at the shadows around him. He looked back down to the grave, wondering what it was that he had just seen. Had any of it actually happened? Had he just really seen that poor woman's final thoughts? Could that have been some strange and elaborate illusion?

"Was that real?"

He began to wonder if he was 'cracking up' and losing his grip on reality. Whatever reality happened to be at this point. There he was, still in that decrepit cemetery, and again walking along that same naturally maintained pathway. He began to wonder and mumble to himself as he looked at his surroundings.

"How did I get here? I know that I was doing something, but I can't remember what it was. It's like I was supposed to have an appointment or something like that. I feel like I was on my way to something, I just can't remember what it was."

His mumbles were cut short when he began to hear a voice, like a whispering in the slight breeze as it softly rustled the ivy leaves against the stone. It sounded as if it were so distant, miles away, and as much as he tried, he couldn't determine from which direction it was coming from. He couldn't make out the words that it was saying, or even if it were speaking at all, yet still he was drawn by it. He slowly crept through the falling brush until he reached a small clearing surrounded by willow trees and Spanish moss. There in the center of the clearing stood just a simple tombstone, no carvings or designs, reminiscent to the first one that he had seen earlier, but not as aged and worn. As he came closer to the grave, he could hear the voice that had been whispering to him.

Richard 'Richie' Polanski
1984–2008

Boston, Massachusetts

"Death is an eventuality. Unreasoning. Unflinching. Unstoppable. It has always been a matter of how and why…when was never a concern for me. If death was coming, all that you could do at that point was decide how you would die. Would it be screaming in terror? Would it be cowering in fear? Would it be calm, still and unwavering? Would you be compromising yourself? On the other hand, perhaps you were a willing sacrifice to the chances of fate?"

He watched the man as he stood there in his bathroom, wiping away the steam that had built up on his mirror. He began to look around at the simple-styled bathroom that he was now standing in; a faded tile floor, cast iron bathtub, a classic porcelain toilet, and an aged wicker hamper were all that he saw. He stood there and watched as the man began to cover his face in shaving cream, and as he unfolded the pressed-steel straight razor, and began to slowly trim and groom himself.

"There are certain exceptions to this rule, as there always are, and one is freewill. You can choose your own time and manner of your death, if you so wished. Every day that you take a breath, you can choose to stop. The most awesome power that humans have found in our petty, little existence: the power to end life. Some die from caused circumstance: a guy robs a bank, and is in turn shot and killed by the police. Cause and effect, and a victim of his own crafting and situation. Some begin a high-speed chase in hopes of not making it through the climactic crash, which ultimately ends

14

the interest of the general public, and resigns to becoming just another statistic."

He stood there, listening and watching each stroke of the razor against the man's neck, and each rinse and wipe of its blade.

"Some enter a state of inebriation so deep, that you resort to your simplest needs, emotions, and motivations. And once you find your final moves in your mind, nothing can be said to you by anyone that you know, that will sway your course and actions. Nothing that they can say will stop you from starting a fight, or running off into the night. Then one day it hits you…bang! Final Solution. A split-second decision that forces a lifetime of pains, doubts, conflicts, anxieties, questions, hopes, wants, failures, misdeeds and well-meant gestures together. All at once. All for you.

"And in that moment, you become something more than what you have ever known, while still feeling like the smallest blip to have ever appeared on the radars of every sentient creature that has had the chaotic chance to have crossed paths with you along the road of theirs. I've become very familiar with it all. I decided when I was 16, that I would live the rest of my life with the images and memories of one single event. An event that changed my life, and once done and over with, would leave me forever changed in every way."

He began to see the bathroom fade away with the words of the man, morphing into the various locations and people of his childhood home.

"Danny was by far one of my favorite friends to be around on a Saturday night. He could show up with a guitar and start a group music night at the coffee house, or you might spot him at the train station after closing, engaged in a Kendo stick battle that began because he and his 'roommate' (flop mate is a better description) were watching old Samurai movies on a TV marathon and figured, 'Since we got 'em…'

"He had a sharp tongue and idolized the Blues Brothers. He kept telling me: 'I get behind Elwood because…' then he began to sing, smiling with a curl in his cheek, and an eyebrow rose up. 'Jake gets the spotlight in the songs most of the time,

Elwood is just stuck dancing.' He stopped one time and looked me clear in the eyes with such a wonder, looking torn then relieved. Shrugging his shoulders, he said, 'Then again, Jake doesn't have a harmonica.' Danny dazzling us with his logical humor."

He began to look around as he now noticed that he was standing in the man's bedroom as he began to fit himself with his best-looking suit, taking great care not to stain or wrinkle it. And as he dressed himself in his finest elegance, again the stranger found himself witnessing this strange and uncomfortable scene.

"He came to me on Devil's Night, the night before Halloween, and said that he wanted a favor. He decided that he wanted to kill himself. I was completely taken back; it was something that I never really considered hearing from him. We talked for hours; we talked about everything, because we were friends. He told me his reasons, and they shall always be for him and me. At that time, with those circumstances, with his options…he weighed them…and chose. He had decided that all of the problems that were facing him at the time, were problems that would last for years, outlasting any meaningful life change. And no matter how hard he tried to avoid them, confront them, or remedy them, they would always remain behind to alter and distract him, before destroying him."

The stranger watched as the man walked back into his bathroom, as he began to straighten his tie, and dab on his cologne. He watched as he made the last adjustments to himself, and as he picked up the straight razor that was now laying next to the sink.

"I love him and miss him because he was my friend, but I hold no other personal feelings toward it all. His life, his choices…not my life, not my choice. He wanted me to stay with him while he did it, because he said that he thought it was the saddest thing for somebody to have to die alone. So, I stayed, and I made sure that the last thing that he saw was a friend, when (as strange as this may sound to those who have never reached bottom) he needed one the most."

He watched as the razor sliced open the man's wrists, and listened as his skin parted from itself, sounding as if his very flesh were being ripped from him.

"He was right about one thing though...nobody should have to die alone."

"What does it say about someone who is such a good friend that they sit through a suicide, while they themselves are entertaining the very same thoughts. Battling equally dark demons of their own and considering the possibility of ending it all and not having to worry anymore about societies or dramas or pains. What does it say about someone who was such a good friend that he mentioned your suicide in his very own suicide letter? He could have said anything about anyone, he could have blamed the world for all his problems, he could have taken it all out on everyone else. But what does he choose to write about in his final moments, a friend. A friend that meant so much to him, that even in his last minutes of life, his friend was within his mind. I would say that is one hell of a friendship."

"What is this? Is this some sort of sick game? What is the purpose of this? Why are you doing this?"

The stranger began to come accustomed to the sound of his own voice reverberating only off the stones around him, and never receiving a reply. He began to wonder what exactly was going on to him. He was seeing these people's lives, he could hear their voices, he could see their homes, knew their friends and family members' names. He could feel everything; he could feel all of it.

"Fine, don't answer me then. What the hell is this place?"

So many thoughts began to wind their way through the stranger's head as he tried to contemplate what it was that was happening. Could he just be having a very vivid dream, with a complex mixture of sights, sounds, and characters? Could he be having some unbelievable reaction to some strange and obscure drug that caused amnesia and hallucinations? Had he fallen somewhere, hitting his head, causing him to wander about in the middle of the night, only to regain consciousness trapped within some abandoned church's graveyard?

He continued to mutter and mumble to himself as he tried to find some sort of path that would lead him out of his current situation. And it wasn't long before he found himself next to a small pond, scattered with lily pads and reeds along its edges.

And there laying right along the edge of the pond's bank, lay a stone coffin, exposed at its base by the water erosion of the pond. It was a hauntingly beautiful sight, something almost that you would expect to see in some great vampire novel set in New Orleans in the 18th century. It was beautiful, and still so out of place. Every image that he could see before him was a beautiful image and appropriate to its surroundings aesthetically, but when seen together, they just could not compliment themselves. None of them looked to be in the right scene or setting, yet there they were laid before him.

And as he stood there looking about this macabre scene before him, again he began to hear a whisper. But it was not the same whisper as before, its voice was different, eerie and filled with air. It sounded as if it were trying to talk over itself, clamoring for the chance to tell its tale. Again, he couldn't tell where it was coming from or how far away it was, its voice had no distance to it. As the man looked around, attempting to either understand what it was that he was becoming a part of, or to prepare for the sense overload that he was about to endure...his gaze flowed down. There sat the headstone.

Jack Mathew Trail
1952–1988

Laughlin, Nevada

"Buy 2, Get 1 FREE'…'Prime Rib $4.99'…'Best Collection Anywhere'…'World Famous'…what a bunch of whores. Billboards as far as the eye can see, all the advertising that you could ever want. And off they go like sheep into the wolf's den. 'Next Exit'…'5 Miles Left'…and off they go. It is so simple to spot the weak ones, especially out here, all that you have to do is sit back and wait…and watch."

As he sat there dictating inside my head, the thoughts that filled his, the stranger found himself behind the wheel of a 1986 Chevy caprice classic, looking at the man's eyes in the rearview mirror. The man swept his hair to the side, done in some sad attempt to be vain, as his voice came back.

"Out of state plates…vacationers, mini-van with only one kid in the back…parents live well enough, the overachievers I'll bet. They are always insured but usually only have credit cards…easy way to get caught. 2-Door Coupe, a little beat up, three teenagers…even easier target…but usually broke and high, just out looking to have a little fun. But this one here, this one looks promising…"

There, the man's focus landed upon young blonde woman driving a beat up yellow pinto. Her face looked sad but calm, as if she were lost in her own train of thought.

"Solo driver…out of state plates…junk in the back seat…off to start a new beginning somewhere, maybe with friends, maybe with family, or maybe just striking out on her own, trying to find her way. Just imagine how hard this girl's life must have been, having to deal with one rejection after another, one failed relationship after another. All she wants is to be able to start over somewhere that nobody knows who she is, who know nothing of her last life."

The stranger could feel his hands reach down to the ignition key and begin to turn the engine over. He sat there for a brief moment, adjusting his mirrors and pulling his car on to the highway, emerging from its hide behind the roadside billboard.

"It's a sweet idea actually, and a sweet thought…too bad it won't work out for you. I'm sure that it would have been nice, but it's nearly nightfall, and you have been going for quite some time now little lady. I think that it is just about time for a little rest up at the rest stop down the highway."

A slight chuckle came out of the man's mouth as he reached to the console on his dash, and flipped on his blue lights, smiling even more when noticing that the car in front of him was pulling over.

"Like I said: It's easy to spot the weak ones…especially out here."

Barbara Joan Curry
1961–1986

Harrisburg, Virginia

"I was never meant for this life; I know that now. A random collection of mistakes and leftovers; I did the best I could with what I was given. I was not meant for this; I know that now. Never quite feeling like I had a place in any society that I tried to live in, merely walking around blending in with the scenery. I was meant for other things, things far away from here. Most anywhere is a place where dreams can happen for you, unless you find yourself stuck in your own private nightmare, helpless, lost, and alone and confused with no sign of waking up."

The stranger could only listen and watch as the faded yellow pinto passed a road sign advertising for a hotel and buffet a few miles down the road. He began to notice all of the items that were scattered and packaged on his back seat, some in boxes, others in bags. He started to see an entire life packed up and miniaturized to fit into the backseat of a small hatchback.

"That would be merciful, and if there is one thing known above all else, it is this: life is unmerciful. Either you take what is dealt to you, or...you ensure your own happiness & future by any means necessary. Sometimes all you need to do in your life is make a change, maybe a new job, maybe a new home. Sometimes you just need to make yourself a new life."

There in the night sky, he began to focus on the stars and light clouds that were out on this night. He was taking in the feeling of the warm desert air, and hearing Tom Petty on her radio.

"I just hope and pray that I am making the right choice. Going somewhere that you don't know and have nobody to contact if you need things? Having to learn a new job and a new city without the benefit of a friend or trusted colleague to help guide you along the way, so you don't get lost? It's a big gamble to take, but it's always the big gambles that pay off. And when you've got nothing left to lose and everything to gain, sometimes you just have to take the chance that you're given and hope for the best."

And in that moment of complete happiness, contentment, and clarity, his gaze was lifted to her rear-view mirror.

"Lights? Police? What did I do now?"

"How sad and strange a situation for our little couple to come to know each other, and for so brief of a time. A woman, beaten, pushed around like a veritable doormat in relationships, a failure in everything that she has ever attempted. Starting new adventures and attempting a new life where nobody knows her, where she has no history, and she can be whomever she chooses to be. A woman who is trying to rebuild a life that she has come to regret. A truly noble and lifesaving cause.

"Unfortunately, she happened to come across a man who worked for the Nevada Highway Patrol, who had also pulled over nine other women over the past five years, all of whom were now either on a missing poster or buried in the ground. He would meet his end two years later, at the tip of a needle in the state execution chamber. As it turned out, the one person that this woman had expected to help her and protect her, only saw the number ten in his head."

"What does any of this have to do with me?" The stranger stood from his position by the tombstone. "Why are you doing this to me? Are you enjoying this?" He continued to walk again through the glades, and again he began to not only talk to himself, but to hear the voices begin to rise up all around him. It overwhelmed him and flowed through him, not louder than a whisper and yet still so loud that it felt like an assault upon his senses. With every sight that he continued to witness, his thoughts became darker and more filled with fear and bewilderment. He had begun to disregard the questions of how and why he was enduring these visions, and began then to just walk.

"This is too much. If this is real, if I truly am seeing these things, then something is definitely off. I just don't know what it is." The stranger began to wipe the sweat off of his face, or at least what he felt as sweat; what it was he didn't know, nor could he identify, and yet on he walked with the same casual swagger and a feeling of trepidation. "This isn't normal; I know that much. But I still have no idea what is going on, and I'm almost afraid to continue any of this."

Absorbing and contemplating everything that he was experiencing, as he made his way through the trees. The voices never cease, always droning in the background of the static atmosphere. Sounds upon sounds blending and weaving into each other as the stranger passed headstone after headstone.

That is when he saw where the voices were coming from. There before him, laid in a nearly baron patch of land laid at least fifty graves, all nameless and unmarked. No headstone to be found among any of them, save one.

"What monstrosity is this?"

Sitting at the head of the plots, as if leading some great flock in a motivational rally cry, stood a worn and weathered statue of a person, resembling something of a preacher or civic figure.

Becky Michelle Connors
1898–1969

Dallas, Texas

"There is a brief moment just before death takes you where time stands still and loses all its meaning. A single second stretches on for a lifetime, yet at the same time becomes fleeting and disappears forever. That single moment in time becomes the most important to you...after the 'yes' and just before the plunge. That single moment becomes more memorable than any other that you have ever had, more painful than any that you have ever had, calmer...clearer...more important than anything else. Because in that brief moment of time, you become a god, with the power to control and manipulate, to create life...and to take it. It is the closest that you will ever reach toward immortality, and just as quickly as it was given to you, it is taken away by your very own hand. It is hard for most to understand, impossible for others...taboo for nearly all, something that is shied from, if even acknowledged at all. But that is because they have never found themselves faced with that decision or those circumstances."

As she stood there, surrounded by the friends and families of her community, the stranger began to watch the intensity at which these people were listening to her, the eagerness to hear and discuss the views that she was expressing.

"There are those out there who have reached the edge, looked beyond it to see oblivion, and turned back. Perhaps from fear of death, or maybe for love of life, or maybe they were simply too afraid of the unknown to try and venture into it. They never reached the depths of pain and sorrow and fear and dread that we did, they never became so hollow and empty inside that every joy and passion within their lives turned to ash in their mouths. No, they found a reason to step back from the edge, however small or earth shattering it may have been to them. But then as time goes on they begin to forget what it was that drove them to the edge in the first place. They hide it, bury it, forget about it, refuse to acknowledge that it even exists, and in that moment, they finally become themselves. They feel alive for the first time in their lives, renewed and with a purpose."

The stranger stood there watching this oratory spectacle that was going on before him, watching the crowd of people nod and smile their heads. Some of the older women in the back could be heard mumbling 'how true' her statements were as they shook their heads in a slight display of sadness and pain.

"Not all are as fortunate as they, not all are able to find that rainbow after the storm...that one simple thing that makes it all worth it. Not all of us are fortunate enough to become one of the truly living, one of the enlightened people. For the majority of those who do make their way to the edge and decide to take that final leap, there is only oblivion and darkness, the end of all things for them."

Within the brief pause of her words, children and animals could be heard playing in the distant background, chasing each other and giggling along the way every time that they heard the dogs bark. It was within that brief moment in time, that he realized he was looking at families, an entire community held together by each other, involved with each other's lives, and raising their families with all of the same values that they had worked hard to achieve.

"But every once in a while, you can find those who made it to the edge, took the leap...and came back. For those, nothing within their world will ever be as it was before. They taste things differently, they speak differently, they listen differently. They have been to the other side and made the journey back...through the darkness, through the end of it all. They change, from that one brief moment, nearly every aspect of their lives and at times even their essence that makes them an individual.

"Fear is the most common thing to change first. Once back to the world of the living, they come to realize that they no longer have any, no fear of anyone or anything. Nearly every human is given, or develops, a natural fear towards death, ensuring that they avoid anything that might help to rush them toward an end. The main drive of that fear is a love and want for life, and to have more and to keep it. But for those who come back without the fear, there are no limits to what can be achieved. There is no fear to hold them back, no doubt to cloud their judgment…only a solid desire and a will of stone. The greatest fear that nearly everybody suffers from is the fear that they might lose something, be it property, or possessions, or even their own lives. Remove the fear and all you are left with is the will and desire to achieve all that is yours."

He watched as they all began to nod in agreement and clap and praise her. Everyone was focused on this old woman, even while they were serving the food to the tables spread across the field, and pouring the drinks for all of the children.

"It is only after you have lost everything that you are finally free to accomplish anything; why is there a reason to fear the loss of something that is trivial? Possessions can be reclaimed, property can be re-bought…they are mere objects, some for pleasure, some for need…but all replaceable. To forfeit ambition for fear of losing simple trinkets and bobbles is illogical in the endeavor to become more than just you. Your pictures are not you…your house is not you…your wardrobe, books, electronics, and every other item that you have collected over the years because they were 'so me'…are not you. They are objects, nothing more; a sorted collection of knick-knacks and social trophies of distinction that in the end amount to absolutely nothing…except to you."

The applause rang out from within the crowd, causing every man and woman to begin engaging in the spectacle that was going on. Children were held in their parent's arms, waiving and laughing.

"When you are finally able to realize that your 'life' is not life, and that at any moment it can all be taken away from you without reasoning or cause, then you will finally be able to view the world through a new set of eyes and judge with a new logic of rationale. Most people can't do that though, they don't have any need or want to. They are content with what little they have been given to work with.

"They like their house, and their car, and their jobs too much to even consider risking any of them...not even for the chance at something greater. So, they sit there, day after day, month after month, year after year, growing more and more complacent, giving no thought as to what could happen to every little thing that they have collected together as they try to define who it is that they really are. Sometimes you hear about them, those who lost everything, all that they held so tightly to and fought so hard for. They go through the motions of anger, depression, regret...and for us, the survivors, they become an encouragement. We sit back quietly and watch as these 'civilized' people begin to break down, clutching at any sign of safety or 'normality' that they can find as they fall deeper and deeper into the realm of the hopeless."

Men and women could be seen placing a hand on their chest, raising their other hand toward the sky, seeming reminiscent of some gospel sermon, as men could be seen shacking their fists in anger and frustration.

"They vindicate our reasoning for finding the edge, and asking: 'Yes...or...no?' We watch like voyeurs as they deteriorate into a mere shadow of their former self until finally...they say 'Yes'. Needless pain, needless heartaches, creating an entirely new dimension of emotions to battle on the way to their end, and in more cases than not, helping to push that once sane and rational person into the place where they dare not dwell. Why surround yourself with trappings that can, and in some chances, do end up becoming the very driving cause that pushes you toward your own self-made ending?"

He stood there and watched as she raised her glass in a toast to the community, giving a show of comradery and unity as the families and children all raised theirs in return, smiling and drinking.

"It is no different than smoking cigarettes for 30 years, knowing that they could kill you only to act surprised and outraged when you are told that the cancer spreading through your lungs will kill you within a year. Be it directly or indirectly, you designed a means, and an opportunity for your own death. No different than an addict who knows that each time that they indulge in their vice, that they could end up closing their eyes for the last time…and all for their pursuit of happiness, pleasure and release. When you surround yourself with memories, devices, and distractions and then give them meaning, you are simply engineering the tools and weapons of your own doom.

"You become attached to them so much that you begin to believe that those simple few things that helped to create who you are, are the only things in your life that matter. And when you lose them all, you lose your way. No more hope, no more meaning, no more identity. Then…you have nothing left to live for. Not life; you decided to turn your life into items that could be taken or destroyed, now lo and behold, that is exactly the state they are now in."

The crowd just stood there, now looking more vacant and devoid of any more emotion. There was no laughter from the children, no agreements from the older women in the back, no cheers from the men, as one by one they each slowly began to collapse. Some laid upon the tables, others across the field, all while the dogs barked and ran around the bodies that were now strewn across the ground.

"It is only when we have nothing left to lose that we are the most free, no more trappings, no more fear of loss, no more worries of image…just simple and complete freedom to live. Lose everything…find your way to the edge…take a deep breath…and say: 'Yes'."

Can you imagine? Can you imagine the sight and spectacle of that woman? Standing there in the garden, surrounded by your friends and family, fellow like-minded people, all praising this woman. Filling their bellies, and enjoying their freedoms of life, even as the punch was stirred and distributed. The poison works quickly, and spares none; mothers, fathers, brothers, daughters, and friends alike are all subject to its effects.

What kind of power could that woman have had to entrance an entire community? To contort and abuse their minds and wants and lives, using nothing more than the power of her words. Cult personalities often tend to be great oratories for their own beliefs and voicing their views upon the world and its people. They have even shown us, that throughout our own histories, they can enrapture and captivate even the most doubting skeptic, driving him to step out of himself and to follow and devote himself to a single person and their vision of the world, becoming something of a disciple. It is a very powerful experience.

"This is unbelievable, who could do such a thing? How could people be so blind and sheepishly willing to follow someone who is obviously insane?"

Not all who rant, and rave are always ill or mentally unbalanced.

"So, it would seem."

The man decided to try and just walk through the wall of trees and moss that stood before him, no longer caring if he were to find a way out of this hellish nightmare he was experiencing. No paths, no clearings, no ponds; for mile after mile, all the stranger could see were trees, bushes, vines and moss. He began to think that he had finally managed to escape from that unholy place. And as he thought that, he looked through the trees, he saw an old farmhouse, looking not unlike an old plantation that had been neglected after the war. As he looked at the house, he began to witness a new horrific scene unfold before him.

This was something new, not something that he had witnessed or felt before. There were no voices to be heard, except those mixed within the sounds that he was now hearing from inside of the house.

Nemesis

From outside the dilapidated farmhouse, only one light could be seen burning through its silhouette, illuminating the room in front of him. He could see a fireplace lit ablaze and roaring, surrounded by rustic and simplistic décor, and from that same room you could hear the screams of a young man.

He tried to look around but was unable to see anything through the burlap bag that had been placed over his head. Strange sounds, he wasn't home…there was a strange feel to the room, warm and yet still chilly. He could feel the floor, old and splintered hardwood, and with his foot, he could feel the waves of heat radiating from the fireplace, as he worked to orientate himself to his new surroundings.

He could hear a strange sound in between the random crackling of the smoldering logs at his side, it sounded to him like an eerie creaking sound, reminding him almost of his grandmother's old rocking chair. He tried to focus his eyes on the glow from the fire, turning and spinning his head around in a frenzied daze.

"Hello? What is this? Hello?"

His thoughts were cut short when that once strange and eerie creaking sound, suddenly stopped. The boy froze, that was all that he could do, that and feel the pulse of his heart begin to beat franticly, followed swiftly by hyperventilating while trying to search for some composure in his fearful haze. Then he heard the sound of boots beginning to walk a slow and steady pace toward him. His body began to go into a near 'overloaded' state, flashing images and fears through his head, while the sounds of the boots continued to come closer to him. The boots stopped, and as they did…so did his breathing.

The man pulled the bag off of the boy's head, showing his confused and still drugged state. He was tied to the chair, each wrist to each armrest, and each ankle to each leg. His waist was tied to the back of the chair, intertwining with the ropes that held his arms and chest to the backrest. He was in his early 20s, unkempt, and didn't really stand out in a good way, or a bad. He was a rather standard looking boy, by any account of those who had met him, someone who has managed to get by for most of their life on charm and wit.

The man stood there for a brief moment as he began to fold the bag in a neat, yet hapless way, looking at the boy as he sat there, showing a range of emotions across his face, from wonder and curiosity, to disgust and contempt. He walked over to a little trolley cart that had a pitcher of water and glasses on it, and began to pour out a glass for the boy.

The boy tried to focus his eyes as he saw the man turn to him, and begin walking. All the while, still carrying the glass of water, and never taking his eyes off of the boy.

"Would you like some water?"

The boy sat there with a petrified stare at the man, caught completely off guard by his question, combined with the situation that he could now begin to see…and feel. He knew that he was in very real danger, and he also knew that he had to try and get out of this mess. But he didn't know what the man had planned for him, all that he knew was that whatever it happened to be, it would not end well for him. The man just stood there looking at the boy as he began to show signs of 'coming to', all the while, still holding the glass of water out toward the boy. He waited a moment, holding a domineering gaze over the boy, until he grew tired of their little staring game.

"No? Well, maybe you'll care for some later."

The man began to walk to a small stand that was set next to the boy's chair, placing the glass of water on it, and a bent straw into the glass. The boy was speechless as he watched the man return to his rocking chair, and sit; locked together in a strange wonder about their current situation, the boy looking at the man, and the man looking back at the boy.

The boy began to see the ropes that were keeping him bound to this wooden and steel beast that was bolted to the floor. He began to try and tug and pull on his ropes, attempting to lift his feet and hands, but all to no avail. After only seconds of fighting with his confinement, he stopped and began to look around at the wooden shack of a room that he was in. He could tell that the house was old, at least 200 years, and he could see out of the small window behind him, that from where he was now at…there was no chance of anybody finding him.

"Who are you? Why are you doing this to me?"

The man just sat there, rocking, looking…thinking.

"Why are you doing this? Why am I here! Why won't you answer me?"

The boy lowered his head and looked as though he was going to begin to cry, but didn't. He simply sat there shaking his head, while under his breath giving sarcastic laughs mixed with slight whimpers.

"There, now that we are all calm, no tantrums, no 'pities' or whining…"

"WHAT?"

"I guess we still have some left after all."

The man continued to rock in his chair as the boy began to vent; one slur after another the boy only fueled the man's purpose and drive, confirming for him everything that he believed that was wrong with society, people, and this boy. As the boy finished his rant, he began to calm and tire.

"Why are you doing this to me?"

"Now, I know that you don't look the brightest, but I know that you cannot be that ignorant, son."

"What?"

"You know why your here, just like you know why you do the things that you do. You do it, because you are a devil, boy."

"A WHAT?"

"You heard me, you heard me just fine."

"A devil? Are you insane!"

"It is not your fault that you were born a devil. It's not your fault that society failed you, that people failed you…but it is your fault for taking it and feeding it. The world did not feed your evil boy…you chose to do that all by yourself."

"What are you talking about…?"

"You knew that it was wrong to steal from your neighbors when they went away on a vacation, but you did it anyways…"

"My wha…"

The boy sat stunned as the man continued to preach off every misdeed that he had done, as if he had followed him his entire life, like some sort of deranged fan.

"…you knew that it was wrong to torture your little puppy dog, when he was so helpless, and you were so strong, but you did it anyways. You knew that it was wrong to destroy someone else's life, their name, their home…all because you wanted to be with their women, but you did it anyways…"

The man stood from his chair and began to walk toward the boy, stopping in the center of the room, illuminating a new level of fear and anxiety to the boy's mind, as he stood in the red and orange glow of the fireplace. His shadow cast across the wall in an almost demonic fashion, with no real or defined edges, acting as if it had a will of its own to cast as it saw fit, as it danced across the walls and rafters.

"I saw what you were doing there, boy. What you was doing out there tonight."

"Wha…"

"I saw it all…what were you doing with that girl there, boy?"

The boy was frozen with disbelief and confusion.

"Huh? No explanation for that? No defense against it, against such vile acts?"

"What are you talking about?"

"Don't you know that them little girls, like that one that you were with…are harlots? They are the whores of Babylon, the beasts of Sodom and Gomorrah."

"Harlots!"

"You know that, don't ya boy?"

"What the…what fucking century are you from man? You're a fucking nut!!! Let me go! Let…"

"Fu…" The man's face turned from resolve and belief to disgust and frustration. "Young man, there are very few things in this world that are known by everybody, and manners are one of them."

"Manners! You sick fuck!"

33

His torrent of rage was interrupted by a swift backhand to his jaw. The hit struck him so hard, as if he had just been smashed in the face with a brick. The boy tried to focus on anything besides the pain, as the old man began to walk past him until stopping at a wooden table behind the boy. As he pulled off a sheet that covered the table, he revealed a rather intimidating collection of tools and 'toys' for him to share with his newly acquired friend.

"You drugged me, kidnapped me, tied me up, beat me... What the fuck are you talking about, manners!"

He reached for one of the syringes that laid on the table. As he picked it up, his back turned to the boy, he began to educate him on his philosophy towards manners.

"Every parent teaches their child about manners...well, every decent parent anyways. And it's not because they want their children to just be respectful to others, or even to play nice with the other kids..."

He began to turn around, exposing to the boy...the syringe. The boy could do nothing but sit there, exhausted, confused, watching as the man began to walk toward him; slowly making his way to the boy's arm.

"...it's because they don't want their child to do or say anything that would be against them. No parent wants to hear their child screaming obscenities at them, but they still do it and even allow it to happen, all because they weren't strong enough to become parents in the first place. You have to be strict with your children..."

"I don't have children! What the hell are you talking about?"

The man smiled slightly, using only the corner of his mouth, as he injected the boy with his homemade sedative.

"...it takes a village, my boy...we all have to do our part."

He awoke later, unsure of where he was, how long he had been laying there passed out; he knew that his eyes were open, but in every direction, there was nothing to see, only the pitch-black darkness. He tried to lift his hands when he felt the cold iron manacles stop him in his tracks, the sounds of the chains that held them to the ground were the only sounds that he could hear. He sat there on the floor in the dark, trying to struggle his way free, all the while screaming for a savior who might be in the area.

"Hey! HELP! HELP ME! PLEASE! HELP…"

From the darkness came a voice…

"Not so loud!"

All that the boy could do was sit there frozen, his eyes scanning in futility against the black veil around him. That wasn't his voice, nor was it the voice of the old man. He could almost swear that it was the voice of another child, maybe in their teens.

"Yelling won't do any good. The only people who *can* hear you have no interest in saving you. So, there's no point in trying; all you're going to do is hurt yourself and give me a headache."

The boy sat there, trying to wrap his little bit of rationale around it all; it was another boy, of that he was certain. But he still had no answers as to where he was, or for that matter, who was talking to him.

"Help me, please?"

There was no reply, just the soft scraping of the chains against the stone floor…and then, silence. The fear struck him like a flash of lightning, and in that instant, he knew what lay ahead of him. He began to feel the energy vanish from the room, and it began to feel cold and very empty.

"I can't help you, I am sorry for that…I can't even help myself."

The sniffling and weak tears slowly stopped; wiping his nose and eyes, he tried to compose himself enough to talk.

"How long have you been here?"

There was a brief moment of silence, which began to worry the boy…silence before an answer to a serious question was never a good thing. When out of the darkness came the voice again.

"I couldn't honestly tell you…"

The boy sat there listening curiously and intently, hoping to gain some understanding of his present situation.

"I couldn't even tell you the last time that I saw a light that wasn't in my dreams. What I can tell you is that you aren't the first person that I've talked to here, and I fear that you won't be the last."

"There have been others?"

"A few. I don't know why they bring us here, or even *what* 'here' is, but I know that I've been here long enough to have some rather interesting conversations, at a length at times, with some fascinating people. We never exchanged names or personal information as you would with your friends or anything, but we would talk about our adventures, our lives, our regrets, our hobbies…"

The boy could hear chains beginning to rustle in the distance, but he wasn't able to get an exact idea of where. He tried to listen to the voice, it was slightly soft…

He maybe at a distance, but how big could this place be? he thought to himself.

"…and if they were fortunate to last long enough…we would even talk about our experiences here."

The boy's face began to change from one of concentration and intent, to one of confusion and worry.

"What do you mean, your experiences here? What experiences? What *is* 'here'? And who are you?"

There was a little laughter heard as the voice continued to educate his 'new-found friend' to the ways of his new home. The laughter, however, was not a sound of humor or irony, but rather the sound of defeat and a dark sarcasm, which worried the boy as he sat there and listened to his mystery companion.

"I am sorry, where are my manners? I am…me, and that is all that I am. I am me and you are you."

The boy looked confused by the voice's remarks, unable to decide exactly what it was that the voice was trying to tell him.

"That's all?"

"Does anything else really matter anymore down here? Whoever you were before…is already gone, he was left with everyone else out there, in the world. Down here, life is a bit…simpler, so to speak."

"Simpler? What the hell is so simple about any of this?"

As he spoke to the boy, without even realizing that he couldn't be seen, or could even see himself for that matter, he raised his arms to their new maximum height before being stopped by the iron chains that held him fast.

"I said, 'so to speak', I never said that what you were in for was going to be simple or easy. Because believe me, it won't be. It never is, not for any of us."

The boy's anger began to shrink back again after hearing him say that.

"…and 'Hell', as you put it, is exactly what is going on."

"What do you mean?"

"Well, did you ever read the Bible when you were a kid?"

"Yeah, so?"

"…do you remember all of the stories about Heaven and Hell, and Judgment Day, and all of that?"

The boy began to feel the fear building, rising; he could feel his core begin to turn cold as he listened to the voice in the dark explain it all to him.

"Well, I still can't tell you if there really is a Heaven because I haven't seen it. But I can tell you that Hell is very real, and you've just entered it."

The boy felt his stomach sink to the floor, he felt sick. What was this person talking about? Judgment Day? What other people? Had there been more before him?

The boy began to rack his brain for some sense of reality, or even an illusion of something real at this point. Anything to distract his mind from what was happening around him.

"This is a real-life 'Hell on Earth', and we are being punished for our sins."

"What are you talking about? What fucking sins?"

"I don't know how he does it, it's like he knows everything about you; all of your fears, all of your pleasures, your pains, your lies, regrets…he knows your entire life. And he seems to be intent on 'punishing' us for our sins, as he sees them. Oh, and I would be careful with the swearing around them...they get really touchy about that."

"...them??? Who is 'them'?"

"Well, I'm sure that you've already met the 'Father', that's what I call him. He was the first one that I remember, he's usually the first for most of the ones that have come through..."

The boy sat up onto his knees, trying to face the general direction that he felt the voice was coming from.

"Although, we do get to go somewhere, I think. It's always hard to remember, but I've been to another house since coming here. I don't like the woman who lives there, she's a horrid old creature that made me feel sick the moment I saw her. She keeps you there, and does things to you... I don't ever want to go back there."

"OK, hang on a second. What are you talking about when you say that others came through, what happened to all of them?"

"...I don't know how or why, but every now and again, I will begin to feel myself get lightheaded, almost like I'm out of breath or something. I can feel myself fading, like I'm entering a dream, and then I wake up here again. I think that they have to be gassing us or something, because it has happened to the others as well. But we can't ever smell it or tell when it will happen."

"And they what...just disappeared?"

"Yeah."

He was stunned, losing every breath and feeling as if he had just been hit in the chest with a hammer... *How could they just...*

"How could they just disappear?"

"Sometimes when I wake up, they're there...and sometimes they're not. What's so hard to understand? See, when they make you go to sleep...things happen to you."

"...what...things?"

"It's kind of hard to explain...it's almost like flashbacks to a dream. You don't remember it until after you wake up..."

His voice became softer, more shaken and somber, more afraid.

"…the only thing that you remember at first, is falling asleep…a deep sleep. One of those sleeps where the hours fly by like seconds; where you have to ask yourself afterwards if you even slept at all. That's when it hits you, the flashes; the memories of what happened to you beginning to break through the drug-induced amnesia. They torture us you know…"

The levels of fear and anxiety that arose within him were no longer able to be measured, as he began to question everything in his life…and how he had got there. He had never felt the mixture of emotions such as this before, all of the fear, the worry, the anxiety, the panic…it was all beginning to become too much for him.

"…they call it '*Purification*', the cleansing of your sins…or the punishment for them at the very least. You wake up sometimes with marks, wounds, or worse…and no idea of where they came from or how you got them. Then you begin to remember little bits and pieces of things, and at first they seem like something that you remembered from a bad dream or something…"

A slight laugh emerges…followed swiftly by exhaling.

"…but it's not a dream. It's real… *They*…are real."

There was only silence then, no words, no exclamations, no questions. He sat there wondering what was going on, what he had just been made a part of, when after a few moments of silence.

"Do you know what *Hell* really is?"

The boy was caught by surprise and had no answer to give in response.

"It's wishing every time that you fell asleep, that you didn't wake up again. Only to wake up and find out that you're still here, you're still alive."

There was nothing that the boy could say now, struck speechless by what he heard. He sat there for what felt like an eternity trying to regain his composure and slow himself to think. Finally, his voice soft, he asked:

"How long have you been here?"

There was no response, only the silence and the dark. Every passing moment felt to him like an eternity, dragging on and delaying the arrival of some great or tragic news. Then he began to hear the chains move ever so slightly.

"I can't remember anymore."

The mist began to creep into the darkened room, slowly but surely making its way toward the residents in the shadows. Once the gas was inhaled, the boy passed out cold, lying motionless on the floor. The boy began to reluctantly wake up in the same chair that he had become familiarized with during his first memory of this cursed house.

"Now…you've got to understand something boy, I'm not doing this because I like it, or because I want to…"

His words broken sharply by the sound of the wooden paddle in his hand, as it fiercely smacked the bottom of the boy's bare foot. He was sure that even the angels above could hear his screams.

"…it's not as though I have some sadistic love for what I do, it is simply something that I have to do. So, I do it."

The smacks seemed to echo louder with each strike, until the boy could no longer fight the calling of unconsciousness.

As the boy's body went limp, the man dropped the paddle and simply stared at him for a brief moment. His eyes, with intense concentration, glancing at limb and body, showing only the faintest sign of distain for the young man that he had just tortured. His thoughts, however brief they may have been about what he had just done, weren't enough to detour him from his course. This was a man of belief. This was a man who called himself a Messenger, and proceeded as an executioner.

"HEY!"

The voice ripped him from his nightmare, and returned him to his reality, which was by far much…much worse. He found himself returned to his darkened dungeon, chained and bruised.

"Hey, are you OK? You were crying in your sleep."

He tried to wipe the saline confessions from his eyes, sputters of breaths and composure seemed to fight his every attempt to answer his shadowed companion. But as he tried to find his thoughts, his attention was torn away to the siring pain that was emanating from his legs.

He screamed as he bent forward, grabbing his legs in sheer pain.

"It was the feet, right? Yeah. I remember when he did that to me...it was unlike anything that I have ever felt before, unlike any pain I have ever had before. The pain has gone away, been gone for some time now...but I still can't walk. I don't imagine that I ever will again, but then again, I don't imagine that I'll be making my way anywhere anytime soon."

He laughed so sadly, already sure of what lay before him.

"Wh-y..."

"I think that he does it so that you can't run away. This way, even if you did manage to get a hand free and give him a good 'whack'...there's no way for you to get away..."

They both sat there in the briefest of silences, contemplating the reality of what was going on.

"There was a girl here a while ago. She sounded so nice, and probably was before she ended up here. He didn't do to her, what he did to us. He cut her Achilles tendon, on both feet. She rolled over in her sleep one time...and I heard it. Apparently, her foot was laying on the floor already, when she decided in her dream to roll her body in the same direction. It sounded bad, really bad; it was as if she had twisted off her own foot. Thankfully, he took her not too long after that, and she never returned."

"Thankfully?"

"After you endure some of the 'punishments' that he puts you through...you can begin to see some deaths as 'mercy killings'. Sometimes you would rather know that they died, rather than knowing that the next time you fall asleep, it would happen again to them. And maybe even worse."

"Mercy killings?"

"I have asked for death, I have prayed for it, but it hasn't shown up yet. I know what I have had to endure, and I know that out of everybody that has ended up down here, that I have been here the longest, which means that he likes me for some reason and wants to keep me around. I know that I cannot endure him for much longer. I'll tell you right now, he never uses the same punishment twice…for him, each time is a new experience."

The gassy mist began to fill his senses again, as the last feeling that he had begun to dissolve and fade away, as his head cracked with its full force upon the stone floor. The boy began to start entertaining the concept of death as he became aware of the events that were unfolding right in front of him. The same house, the same chair, and that man. His eyes began to wander slightly after they began to focus, and locked on to the hammer and nails that the man was now holding.

"Oh God!"

"Now, boy…now is too late to start asking god for help."

The boy felt his heart pound as if it were attempting to escape its chesty confines. His breathing became erratic, jockeying back and forth between a paralyzed fight to claim air and expel it, and the near hysterical state that accompanies hyperventilation. All he could do was watch motionlessly as the man began to move toward him. Step by step, as it echoed off the aged wooden floors, the footsteps of the man began to shock and electrify the boy's senses. The man stopped just in front of the boy, leaned over toward him, and whispered into the boy's ear:

"You know; I am sorry about this boy…but it must be done. You are evil…"

The boy was now crying painfully as he attempted to speak to the man and talk him out of whatever it was that he had planned to do next.

"Please mister…I'm not a devil."

"…and evil must be stamped out."

It was at that moment that the boy felt the dull razor pain of the spiked nail as it was driven into his right hand. Bang after bang, each repetition of the iron hammerhead smacking against that cold, bloody spike, as it was purposefully and securely driven into his hand and chair, drove his senses to madness. The boy screamed out in such agony, the sound of his voice began to reach a fever pitch as he lifted his gaze from his hand to the man. Standing there, arm raised in preparation for another anguishing blow, the boy noticed a glimpse of something, something strange and out of place (even at a time like this). A tiny red dot.

It didn't look like a blood spot, or even a piece of fabric or dye. This was moving, not by much, but moving around the man's chest all the same. Then the sound rang through the air as the projectile raced through the double paned glass window in the kitchen and began to sharply tear through his abdomen. The boy watched as the man was struck back by the bullet, and before the boy could even begin to process what it was that he had just witnessed, a second bullet came flying through the room and pierced the side of the man's head. The boy felt his heart fall from inside of his chest as his body began to exhale and sigh in the most relieved and relaxed fashion it has ever done.

The boy sat there, groggy and bleeding when he began to realize that he wasn't waking up. This sight was far too real and far too graphic for him to have just remembered it in glimpses and cryptic flashes, this just happened…this actually just happened. He was awake, and someone was saving him. He began to yell and scream at the top of his lungs for help, silencing only when he was greeted with the masked face of a police officer.

"It's alright kid, you're going to be just fine. Can we get a medic over here? We have a survivor! You'll be just fine sir; we've got you now."

The boy was relieved that his ordeal was over, but his body was petrified, as stiff and lifeless as the stretcher he was carried to the ambulance on. As the paramedics carted him toward his ambulance, the boy overheard two of the police officers' discussion of the situation around him.

"Well I guess we can finally close this one out."

"It's about damned time too. Twelve years and eight bodies later."

"Hey better late than never. I'm just glad that your guys went in there before he could do anymore harm to that boy over there."

"Yeah, but it wasn't fast enough. That never should have happened to that boy, he never should have had to go through any of that. We should have had him sooner."

"Maybe, but we can't change that now. All we can do now is just be thankful that it's over and he's dead."

"Dead? You didn't hear? He's not dead, at least not yet. That first gut shot went right through him, missed every major organ on its way out. The damnedest thing. That headshot is what put him down. But apparently it wasn't enough, the medic says that he still has a pulse and very faint breathing. The bullet is still in his head. He's definitely down for the count, but he's not out yet."

"So what hospital are they taking him to?"

"Same one as that boy I suspect, after all, it's the only hospital within a 20-mile radius."

The boy still in shock at the events that brought him to now, began to fall deeper into his pain as he heard that the 'Father' was still alive, and would be somewhere close by, as they both healed from their wounds.

"I got things taken care of here, why don't you go on back to the hospital with them and take care of your paperwork there?"

"Yeah, you're probably right. There's not much else I can do here. I'll catch you later."

The boy laid there, letting the multiple meanings of what he had just heard bounce around and echo within his head. And as the doors began to close on the ambulance, the boy looked over at the limp body of the man who had taken such joy and pleasure out of torturing and abusing him. He began to mutter to himself: "I hope you die horribly. I hope you die painfully."

It was in that moment that the boy caught a glimpse of the man's face, and became petrified as he stared at the man's eyes as he rolled them toward the boy…and winked.

Such a horrific experience, what that boy must have endured. And what of the other voice that he heard in his confined home? What of that? What of the man and his mission to cleanse the world of its impurities as he saw them? What a unique and barbaric family to have? And what of that sickening woman, I wonder?

The house began to fade away from view, almost as if it were projected upon a screen of smoke, only to be whisked away by the breeze.

What new and curious things might await you now?

"I'm almost afraid to find out."

As the house disappeared, the stranger could now see a cottage behind the house, something reminding him of a woodsman's hut. It was simple and rustic, with only a single dim light coming from a window at the side of the house. Cautiously, he moved his head to a position where he could see the interior of the house.

Saved

*"...be wary, because the Devil, your adversary walks among you. Yes, he does, and he is doing it at this very moment. He is doing it in your streets, in your schools, in your businesses and in your very own home! *screams of 'no...no' come from the audience* Yes, they do! But you don't want to admit it, you don't even want to acknowledge that it is there...and who could blame you? I couldn't...I wouldn't want the knowledge that someone or something, who was the very epitome of everything that my Lord has told me was right and righteous and good...was just strolling around town, looking, watching, and infecting anybody that I love or care for, with his poisonous lies. That is not what my Lord has taught me... He has taught me to beware of those who are the sinners of Babylon...*cheers and 'amen's shout out*...He taught me to beware of those who would do the Devil's work and attempt to destroy and defile my love and faith in my Lord and Savior! *the revival grows louder, fueling the frenzy of the parish*... He taught me to be righteous in my convictions,*

45

*righteous in my words, and righteous in my actions...*the crowd praising him with 'amen's and 'preach it'*"*

*"Matthew 13:19 tells us, that when anyone hears the word of the Lord and does not understand it, that the evil ones take away their heart...he takes away their heart. *the crowd begins to cry out 'no!'* Now, I don't know about all of you good folks here with me now, and I can't say that I can speak for any of you who are listening to this broadcast at home, or at your work...but I don't exactly like the thought of losing my heart! Do you? *jeers of 'no...no' cry out from the crowd* That doesn't exactly sound like a very good time to me; I happen to like having my feelings, my loves, my passions...that's what makes me who I am! *'hallelujah...amen'* So I chose to fight for the Lord...* 'Amen!'*...I choose to fight for my Savior because of what he has given to me, for my wonderful family and my lovely wife, for my home and my friends...and for all of you who are listening to me right now. *the revival explodes with roaring*"*

The cackle of the woman was sickening as she clapped her hands in a halfhearted way. "That's right preacher, that's right. You tell it like it is," her voice cutting in between her raspy breaths.

*"We must keep our faith in the Lord in the dark times that are ahead of us, we must keep our faith in each other and keep our eyes open to any and all that might attempt to ruin and destroy all that our Lord has provided us! *the crowd's jubilee reaches a fever pitch*..."*

As the radio clicks off, the woman struggles to her feet, fighting to lift herself from her chair. She is a large woman, nearly frighteningly looking...creepy to be sure. She begins to shake her head with a worried look of concern... "That man is right on it...there *are* far too many sinners in the world, and nobody seems to care..." She continues her rantings as she walks across the room, shuffling her feet as she goes, "We never seemed to have any problems until they opened up that damned highway, and now anybody who wants to can just 'stop on in'! None of them have any manners…no politeness to give…only corruption, filth, degradation…and death."

Her steps become heavy and slower with every step she takes "…they will try, with all of their might, to try and abuse you, pervert you, and take you away from the love of the Lord…" She stops and reaches down to tear away the burlap cover that laid over the cage…to expose a boy, curled up upon himself in the corner, tears staining his cheeks. She leans down over him, "…but we won't let that happen to you, you're a good boy. It's not your fault…the devil is a tricky beast, but you won't have to worry about that anymore." Her smile is almost sickening, twisted…her eyes are lifeless, with no hint or sign of a soul or rational mind.

The boy looked up at her and watched as she began to rotate herself and begin her shuffled march back to her worn down and 'lived in' chair. He tried to gasp a breath between his cries, "…please…let me go…I want to go home…please…" causing the woman to stop in her tracks. She doesn't turn around, she only turns her head, just far enough to see the small boy pressed against the door of the cage, looking much like a prisoner of war. "My dear sweet, silly child…you are home. You're home with the Lord now…"

The boy began to collapse upon himself and burst into tears as the woman walked back over to the radio…and turned the knob… *'click'*. The voices began to fade in, rising from the static of the old set as she turned to sit back down in her favorite chair, exhaling an exhausted grunt as she leaned back.

"…and they may come to their senses and escape from the snare of the Devil, having been held captive by him to do his will. To save their souls…that is what this is all about…saving souls…"

She became so enwrapped by her preacher, that she never even felt the heart attack as it began to surge through her chest and shoulders. The little boy just sat there and watched it all, becoming filled with confusing paradoxes such as witnessing a person dying and being glad that they are dead. That poor boy…nobody found him for another three months.

By then, obviously, it was far too late to do anything about his situation.

"This is madness! This is sick madness! I've had enough of this… Enough!"

The stranger stood there by the field that once held that disturbed and violent home. And as he stood there, absorbing what he had just seen, his focus was broken by a scream. This was unlike the voices that he had been hearing for most of the night, this was a very clear and very distinct scream. It was a woman's scream. He began to move out into the field where he tried to follow the sounds of shrilling madness. As he made his way through the fields, being whipped by plants and a decayed harvest, he could begin to hear more screams. They were maddening screams, the screams that you make when you are truly afraid and terrified of what you are going through. It is a scream of pure madness and torture.

Then, emerging from the trees as if stumbling across some great Mayan temple buried in a jungle, there it stood. A great building complex, so intimidating and so sterile in its appearance. It loomed over the scenery like some clinical madman with a look of derangement and perversion in its eyes, waiting to see what happens next. From inside the building he could hear the cries again. As he slowly began to walk the hallways, he began to see the people walking the halls, and talking as if he were watching some great and intricate play unfold.

He began to walk the halls and look into the rooms of the patients. He decided to follow an orderly who was walking the halls with a determined and professional air about him. He looked like someone who worked here, or at least knew his way around the building. But every time that he would find himself next to a room, he would look in, and the visions would continue.

Room #30
Rachael's Room

Room #30: Ms. Sanders, Rachael Marie
Patient ID: RS-1138
Reason for Admission: Suicide
Recommendations: The patient is to be given a daily regimen of Anti-Depressant medication, as mandated by the Clark County Courthouse, as part of a Rehabilitation and Wellness Project.

Little by little she felt herself drift off, unable to fight against the weight of her own eyes. Arms bound, tied in the oh-so comfortable hugging fashion that her fellow friends have become all too familiar with, she sat there in her induced haze. The walls were comfortable; every angle felt like a pillow for her heavy head…as she begins to lose her struggle with the sleep. "I do-don't want…to…I'm…not…t-i-r-e-d…" Her eyes slam shut, and her head hangs itself upon her new pillow in the wall as she feels herself begin to slip away.

"Hello? Hello?" *no echo…??? No depth at all? This isn't right, something isn't right here…* "Hello…?" No sound, no reverb to her voice at all, only the flat scream of her voice into the pitch-black void that surrounded her; it enveloped every space around her, showing no definition between any points of reference, no sky…no ground…simply a great void of absolute nothingness. Her voice became more frustrated and softened before her final blow, as she mumbled to herself "…this is some bullshit…" and then she fired…

"HELLO!!!"
There was no time for her to react to the booming echoes that began to fire back at her from every direction… *"HELLO…!!! Hello…!!! HELLO, HELLO, HELLO!!!!!!"* The echoes came at her from every angle and flowed around, and through her very body, assaulting upon every one of her

senses…each individually receiving savage attentions…all at once. Her head felt like it was beginning to swell open, the sounds of the echoes of her voice that seemed to only be heard within her head, with no registration from her ears of any noise at all. As the echoes inside of her head began to pulse and tear from within her skull, she began to cry out and she began to shake, in part from terror, and in part from pain.

She tried to cover her ears with her hands, but the shattering assault of her voiced echoes seemed to pass straight through her hands, as if they weren't even there. She fell to her knees…no 'bang'…no hard landing upon a solid and believable surface, only the feeling of stopping without shock, and feeling held up by a cushion of air. *What is going on!!! Oh God, please… STOP!!! STOP!!!* "STOP!!!" Her voice screaming so hard through her throat, that her pitch began to crack…exposing all of the pain, terror, fear, frustration, and anger that she was experiencing throughout every inch of her.

And just as sharply and frighteningly as it had begun…it stopped. No sound now…only the perfect silence that surrounded her. Her eyes sprang open, her entire body trembling, and slowly feeling disconnected from herself as she fought to slow the hummingbird pace of her breathing…and heart. *Wh-at…the…fuck…?*

"Rachael…over here!" She paused for a moment, trying to register what she had just hear from the void. She was trying to focus her eyes in the darkness, when she saw Robin standing across the street from her; he was a cute boy with red hair and a simple love for Star Wars that none of the other kids in the neighborhood seem to understand, bouncing a smoothly worn basketball on the sidewalk. She couldn't take her eyes off of him… *Robin? What is this? This isn't right, I'm not here, this can't be real…* "Come on Rachael, I wanna show you something…"

"He wanted to show me something…" her voice was soft, calm…painful. *What did he want to show me? What was it…something behind his…* A pause entered her thoughts as she felt herself exhale…*the ducks. He wanted to show me the ducks that had decided to make a little home for themselves in the pond behind his house.* All she could do was sit there on her knees in her front yard and stare at Robin as the tears began to slowly flood her eyes, a small smile crept across her face.

"Rachael...I said I want to show you something..." he yelled out as she watched him begin to run across the suburban street that separated their houses. Then...panic...her voice spiked as her arm outstretched toward Robin, "ROBIN!!!" The Cascadia hit him at 45 mph...and in less time than it took for her to blink...he was gone. She tried to breathe as her hands covered her mouth with so much force, that she felt as though she might rip off her own jaw in her hysteria.

She doubled over crying, her eyes clinched tightly, as if they were trying to prevent any tears from flowing. The sound of the air horn of the big rig as it continued to pass on, began to spin itself around her head...a lot like spinning a marble in a bowl. The sounds of the horn began to drift off into the distance, disbursing itself in every direction. She opened her eyes...only to find herself laying down in a parking lot.

She tried to look around, but the lot was empty with no cars to be seen, only a chain link fence surrounding the perimeter. Two brick buildings stood flanking the parking lot, both four stories tall...both businesses that are closed at this time of night. Her location looked reminiscent of some back-alley bar's parking lot, 'out of the way' and secluded, and poorly neglected. Then she looked up and saw writing on the side of one of the walls...she tried to focus...

The headlights blasted on from behind her, blinding her as she turned to see what was happening. She tried to cover her eyes, but the car's headlights seemed to burn right through her hands. It was a beautiful car, a 1971 Chevelle SS, red with two black racing stripes that stretched across the car like a bandit's mask. "Now come on baby...don't be like that..." the voice was cocky, hardly apologetic...even giggling under his breath as he exhaled the smoke from his menthol Kool. "You know I didn't mean it."

Her eyes began to focus on a well-built figure leaning against the center of the hood, his elbows laying on the stripes as if he were held up by them. The Kool stayed hanging on his lips as he delivered his best 'smooth talker' smile to her, looking more like a rebel reject from a bad '50's movie than a Don Juan. "I'd never do anything to hurt you...I love you. I'm here to protect you."

"Tommy? Oh God no..." She was stunned in disbelief at what she was looking at, and where she was.

"Oh...now baby...is that any way to treat an old friend? Is that any way to treat a lover? That's not very nice." he said with a condescending tone as he took one last drag before flicking his cigarette against the wall. As it sparked against the brick, she could see the smoke venting from behind his teeth as he displayed that sickening grin of his.

She raced to her feet and turned blindly away from him, to run anywhere as long as it was away from him...she couldn't even brace for the impact that hit her as she found herself bouncing off of Tommy's chest, knocking her back to the ground. "You know that's not a very nice way to talk to someone who loves you." She tried to kick herself away from where she was, scrambling to get further away from him as he just stood there watching her from above with a smile on his face.

"Fuck you! You get away from me!" she never saw him move the few feet that separated them as she felt his hand grasp around her throat. She tried to reach for something, anything...but only found herself grabbing onto his arm as his strength alone became the only thing holding her off of the ground. His voice became darker and raspier, as he leaned in closer to her... "I said that wasn't very nice." His face began to change to a perverted version of an attempt at sadness, as he said, "Why do you hurt me like that," and turned his face away from her.

The slap blindsided her and as it hit, she could feel it...as if she was being punched with the full force of his power, across every part of her body. The blows alternated location as they began to pulverize her, inside and out. Her screams flowed through the streets of the market and the train depot behind them, and she screamed harder and louder when she realized that the only sounds that she would hear back from the city around her...were her own cries.

As she opens her eyes...*I'm not...no...what the...what is...*only the darkness...only the void. She began to run in every direction, screaming and hollering for anybody to help her. Her steps never made a sound and in the back of her mind, she even began to wonder: *Am I going...crazy?* She kept running, feeling unable to stop and never running out of energy. *What is this? What is going on? There's nothing here? There's nothing here... There's nothing here...*

From the small window in the door they looked on as Rachael sat with her head leaning against the corner, shaking from side to side while mumbling, "nothing here...nothing here...there's noth-nothing here...nothing here...noth-nothing..." Her eyes, glazed over with tears and devoid of any sign of coherent thought or actions, stared at the wall as if staring over a vast distance.

"So, what happened to this one?" A small metal door that covered the window clicked shut as the two interns stood outside of Rachael's room. The doctor looked at them with their notepads ready and pens in hand, "This case here came from a long history of mental and physical abuse. She suffered a rather harsh life by anyone's standards, and decided one day that she was going to escape from it all."

The eager interns followed the doctor as they continued to walk down the sadly lit corridor, glancing briefly at the various names and conditions written outside of the rooms of the other patients in the north wing. "She decided to open up a few bottles of various narcotics and pain pills, and wash them down with a $400 bottle of French wine." The interns were speechless. After walking behind the doctor in a stunned silence for a brief moment, one of the interns said: "She's lucky to be alive."

The doctor stopped and turned around. "Oh no gentlemen, she succeeded in her endeavor." The interns stopped right where they stood as the doctor began to enlighten them on her case file. "Her boyfriend ended up dialing 9-1-1 just before he bled to death; she had taken one of the steak knives and 'given' it to him…from stem to stern. By the time that the ambulance made it to her she was already beginning to fade, her body was crashing, and the only thing that the paramedics could do was continue their attempts at CPR as they raced to get her back to the hospital."

"Her heart officially stopped less than a minute from the hospital…she was flat lined when they pulled up to the emergency entrance, and remained to be that way even after nearly fifteen minutes of resuscitation. They covered her and placed her with the other unfortunates that were waiting to be moved to the storage freezer down in the morgue. She laid there for 23 minutes, a cold corpse, when all of a sudden she sat up screaming and gasping for breath!" The interns looked at the doctor in complete disbelief, beginning to think to themselves that this was all just some medical prank that the staff played on the 'new guys' to shake them up and mess with them a bit.

"By the time that the nurses got to the gurney where she had been laying…she was gone! They found her wandering the halls of the third floor, mumbling to herself…" he said while motioning back toward her room. "She has been that way ever since. We've ran every test on her that we know of, and yet we still can't explain it. Not only how it is that she survived after such an extensive period of being dead…but how it is that she can even function at all? Roughly seven minutes after death, the brain begins to die. It can't sustain itself without the electricity that the body produces, so it shuts down."

"If you manage to come back, and that is most usually a very big if, then you suffer from various problems: speech impediments, loss of motor control, or…you simply become a 'vegetable' and never move, talk, or react to anything in any way. But she is an exception to the rule: she can speak coherently, she has complete control over her motor functions (in the sense that she can move), and as far as we have been able to tell, she is completely healthy. But for some reason, she is still like…that. It doesn't make any sense in any aspect, regardless how to try to look at it."

The interns stood there briefly, trying to take in everything that the doctor was telling them. "So…has she ever said anything other than that? What was it…? There is nothing here… Has she given any ideas as to what any of it means?" The doctor simply shook his head in a sad display of befuddlement and defeat "No, nothing. The only person who will ever truly know what it is that is going on inside of that poor woman's head…is crazy."

The orderly followed the doctor and new candidates, carrying with him his keys to the cells and doors, and a small tray of medication for one of the patients of the south wing. He loved to listen to the doctor's stories about the patients. After a few years of hearing stories and legends about the various patients that had come under his charge over the years, these little special occasions to hear about their histories and his little twists into their past actions, in order to get a little rise out of the 'new people', was his favorite part of the job. A sad psychological game to play on the new doctors as you acclimatize them to their new charges as 'Medical Caregivers of the North Wing'. He always hated that saying.

Although, sometimes seeing the reactions to the patients' real histories was even more priceless. Watching them try to contemplate how those once sane people could ever have so much damage done to them. The stranger could only find himself following the orderly as he began to wind and turn down hallways and around the darkened corners. Down every hallway, he could see room doors.

"This is beyond strange, this is something completely different."

You could even go so far as to say: "It's crazy…"

"Very cute…"

Room #10
X

Room #10: Mr. Morrison, Xavier Caine

Patient ID: XM-228

Reason for Admission: Aggravated Assault

Additional Notes: Patient's sentence of 15 years, due to Aggravated Assault, to be expedited by the Mainland Sanitarium. Sentencing will be carried out under specialized medical supervision, due to frequent psychotic episodes, and a judicial ruling of 'non-compos mentis'. Patient is schizophrenic and must be sedated if removed from his room.

Recommendations: The patient is to be given a daily regimen of Anti-Psychotic and Anti-Depressant medication, as mandated by the Clark County Courthouse, as part of a Rehabilitation and Wellness Project.

Memories are in the blood, locked, hidden away beneath generations of genetic manipulation and chance. But they are there, surfacing in your dreams, in your emotions…drawing you toward a life that has long since passed. You can learn to listen to them, to listen to your blood, to listen to your memories. They still carry on because they are a part of your very being, passed down from generation to generation, until it all finally culminated into you.

For those who can learn to focus their mind, spirit, and emotions upon that one single concept, they are given the chance to see into the past. Some can remember tearing down the Bastille during the French Revolution, others remember running in fear from the ashes of Pompeii, some remember tyrants, others remember saints. The more proficient you become at listening, the further back you can go; I have only been able to see what I can only guess as, the Dark Ages.

I cannot be certain of a year, but the period is after the start of the second millennium (1,000 A.D.?). I know that I was in the British Isles, or at least what became the British Isles, I know that death was a common visitor and that you were considered a man at a much earlier age than we do now. There were fewer numbers of us then, we didn't have time to play, work and survival was always a priority. I remember learning to shoot a bow, and how to handle a sword, I was taught how to ride a horse, and I remember spending at least a short time sailing somewhere.

The ship was small, no women or children, a few small boys but all of them would make sure you remembered who they were from then on out, if anyone were to try and abuse them or cross them in any way. These boys were tough. I remember about two dozen men aboard the ship with us, all of them worked in some capacity for the captain, attending to certain chores or duties as they were needed, but they also followed their own way...their time on their captain's ship was temporary at best.

I cannot deny the fact that I receive an almost sexual 'release' when I think about killing, but it is not for the victim, but the act itself. It is a bloodlust that is rooted deep within me, as part of a warrior existence. Like a stalker, it waits quietly, waiting, watching, preparing. And when it finally takes hold...there is no other feeling like it; you're no longer you, but something more...something else. For most who kill, whether they have to or not...they tend to go through a throw of emotions, including but not limited to...guilt. But for those who have the bloodlust, it becomes an entirely different creature all together, for those tortured ones...there can never be enough.

As I said, my bloodlust is rooted deep within me. So deep in fact, that I have not only had dreams about these events...not nightmares mind you, but proper dreams, where you feel as close to nirvana and the spirit world as you ever can, without becoming a permanent resident to either one. I have had dreams where I have been in a grassy field, but not green grass, more of a golden color, a soft amber…the kind that you see in Greece and Central Asia a lot.

I'm not alone, very rarely am I alone in my dreams, I am joined by a number of warriors, engaged in an arena of gore. I call them warriors because they fight with blades, and bows, and fists, and knives…they had to feel their enemies as they were also driven by the fight or flight of human nature. Not all of them wanted to be there, you didn't have to see it on their faces or hear it in their voices to know which ones they were. All that you had to do was watch them as they fought.

There were those who had families, homes, and professions elsewhere, and you could tell because they always gave every blow as if it were their last. They fought with such intensity, proving that they had something worth fighting for, and something to go home to. No soldier of fortune or warrior for glory or privilege will ever know that feeling, because all that they ever came to know was their weapon and shield. They were more controlled, attacking quickly, sharply, and always keeping one eye on their enemy, as the other one scanned for his next target. The ones that you could almost feel pity for, at times, were the 'men', a collection of conscripts, fortune hunters, glory seekers, and those who were given the choice of service on the battlefield…or the axe. Those were the easiest to spot within the sea of chaos; impulsive, timid at the first hit (and the second…and the third…), and never able to see what was going on around them…until it struck them hard enough to carve through them.

I have seen myself, standing in that field as the madness went on around me, screaming wildly into the air as if to announce myself through the 'war cry calls' that we had grown so accustomed to hearing. There I stood, knife in one hand, as the other hand held the head of an enemy to my chest. I remember that he was kneeling in front of me, his legs pinned under him…behind mine. I don't remember a sound as it happened, no sound…nothing at all; something reminiscent of listening to an album and hearing that faint moment of static-y silence between each track. I don't remember seeing it either; my eyes were closed at the start, but when it began, I do remember opening them…but there was nothing. Only a dark haze, but colorful somehow… I don't know how to explain it, it was as if the dark was being penetrated by these soft explosions of colorful lights. Nothing that looked like fireworks or anything like that, but more like a random 'twinkle' here and there.

I don't remember any of those details too well…but I remember the feeling. I remember, feeling his blood as it began to flow from his neck, warm at first, then it seemed to cool by the second as it began to stain and cake my hand. I remember feeling his body shutter, not in a struggling sense (he could not struggle by this point), but more like a person who is being electrocuted…just convulsing, looking not unlike a small fish after being plucked from the lake. It didn't last for long, eventually fading away like that feeling across my hand, as his weight began to collapse, until he was no more. No more than one more penance to pay, one more trophy to raise, one more victory to drink to, and one more campaign to close. But that feeling never left me.

That feeling that drove me to push, and charge, and sweep, and kill. That feeling told me to want it, told me to crave it, told me to search it out and to find it where ever it may reside. That feeling that made it possible for me to go back to my people, when others became food for the wolves, vultures, and crows. That bloodlust…it is a cruel mistress to tame, and an even crueler one if denied. It will feed on you daily, tearing down a little piece of you at a time, until eventually it has you again and again…and you must satisfy.

I have not only had dreams about these events that I have taken place in…I also have memories. These are not simply dreams like the others, far from it, these are true memories, remembered as if you were recalling your 12th birthday or your first love. I remember feelings, emotions, details clearer than crystal, and the memories of the life lived at that time. I have knowledge of people, places, events, and cultures that have only lived a fraction of the time that it has taken for our, now grotesquely powerful, civilizations to grow into the established entities that they are. I have memories of impossible sights, and doing impossible things, things to which the likes of the 'Modern' world could not comprehend (nor would they be so inclined to even attempt).

The orderly turned down a hallway that wrapped around a nurse's station as he began to make his way to his patient in need. Seven o'clock every day, like clockwork, 'Mr. Jefferies must have his shots'. It's not just for his benefit, but mostly for the staff's wellbeing. He had been known to lash out on nurses and orderlies whenever he began to slip from his lucid periods, so the hospital decided for the benefit of everybody: that when Mr. Jefferies received his daily dose of medications, that we make sure that he is so doped up, he couldn't breathe without assistance. We were to keep him alive, healthy…and heavily sedated. The orderly began to talk to himself: "Speaking of the devil himself, here we are."

Room #1: Mr. Jefferies, James Lynn
Patient ID: JJ-2583

Reason for Admission:	Murder in the First Degree (4 counts) Aggravated Assault (9 counts) Kidnapping (1 count)
Additional Notes:	Patient has repeatedly attempted suicide by various means including: strangulation, medication overdose (morphine), and self-mutilation. Patient is also prone to violent and raging outbursts toward staff members and medical professionals, resulting in the deaths of at least three staff members and holding a nurse hostage in an attempt to incite a 'death by police' situation for himself. The patient has no will to live and no desire to conquer his afflictions and return to a healthy and productive state of mind.

Recommendations: The patient is to be given a daily regimen of Anti-Psychotic and Anti-Depressant medication, as mandated by the Clark County Courthouse, as part of a Rehabilitation and Wellness Project. The patient is to also be administered a 50cc injection of Thorazine on a daily basis, due to his continued violent activities toward the medical staff of Mainland Sanitarium.

Room Number I

I hate the arguments. They give me headaches, worse these days it seems. It never ends, back and forth, day and night. I'm not even safe in my sleep, because now the arguments continue, with new locations every time, new faces of actors fulfilling their parts...however brief they may be. "I want that... I want this." Endless. Tireless. If there is an escape from the madness, I haven't found it...yet.

I try to do the best that I can to stay neutral about it all, to keep my head about me when the headaches build. But more and more I find myself caring less and less about it all. I find myself letting it all just drift, like deadwood for the soul. I'm tired of the headaches. I'm so tired.

My wits have been scattered to the winds, and I have no one to blame but myself...and me. I don't see him, that's not how it works, at least not for me...but I can hear him. I can hear him as clear as if he were in the same room with me, it's very loud and very clear. I have found myself on a few occasions arguing with him, an absurd idea to be sure, but there I was all the same, trying to convince myself of my own point.

The idea was simple enough: with the right amount of conditioning, enough time, and the right motivation...could a person develop insanity? Was it something that only happens to the unfortunates who are born with it, or develop it through some traumatic event in their life? Could a person, voluntarily and deliberately, go insane of their own free will? It took nearly ten years for any effects to show, although in fairness…I didn't focus on it as a serious endeavor until about three or four years ago.

Before I began, I was a 'normal' person, someone who looked forward to having his house in the suburbs, his wife who is still stunning at 40, and two or three kids that would eventually grow up to reach all of those dreams that were just beyond their father's grasp. All of the things that I had come to know, understand and love throughout my formative years, but as with all things…they change, as did I. I no longer cared about a house in the suburbs. I no longer cared about my wife who was still stunning at 40. I no longer cared about having children, watching them grow, or seeing them surpass me in all the ways that I could hope.

The worst part of it all is that I can no longer tell who is in control of whom. Is it still my body that he happens to possess, or have I merely become a figment of his imagination? Einstein once said: "The question that often drives me hazy…is it I, or the others, that are crazy?" Now I understand what it is that he meant, now I know what it means to not only be afraid of the uncertainty of others…but to be afraid of yourself as well. In the end…the greatest danger to our survival and longevity…is ourselves.

But I am beginning to feel it and see it now: as my memories of an entire lifetime are erased and faded into history, they are being replaced by others. These memories are not mine! I'm not even counting my dreams, these are actual memories I'm living through…and I don't have good dreams anymore anyway. I can feel these, I can remember smells in the air, the feel of the ground beneath my feet. I can close my eyes and recollect moments that I never made, and they are as clear to me as yesterday. And I speak about them in the plural because there are quite a few that have begun to surface themselves. I feel as though my very soul has been replaced; I have no sense of who I am.

The stranger stood there for a brief moment watching the orderly pacify his ward with a swift shot to the arm. The cackle down the hall broke his attention and beckoned him toward it. And there sitting upon the bed in his hospital room, was a man who as far as the stranger could tell, was either focused on something to do with the ceiling above him, or on some figure that the stranger could not see.

Premonitions

"Childhood is over the moment you know you're gonna die." I heard that in a movie once and it has never left me, if anything, it has helped to put certain aspects of my life, beliefs, and philosophies into perspective for me. Powerful words to speak in any context, but death is the one, isn't it? Death is the taboo of our species despite all our barbarism, hedonism, theisms…and other various and colorful 'isms' that humans have placed on themselves because they are too scared to think that they might be all alone. Nothing else, not a soul, not a whisper, not a hint of a fruitful and shining path that we were all told would be waiting for us all.

'I can't be this! I have to be more, I have to be bigger than I am, smarter than I am, more important than I am, and I must be master of all that I survey. This is what it is to be human, this is our purpose.' But after all, there is that chance that they could be right in the fact that I could be wrong. Maybe there is something after everything that we have built and hyped up in our short time on this spinning rock, maybe it's something that is beyond both our understandings. Maybe we're both right…and both wrong. Humility can come at a dear cost, and the way that you govern and manipulate your life, in order to bring you the wealth that you craved as a child, or the house that you saw once on a cover of a magazine and cried out in your solitary mind: 'They're living in my house! I should show up there and let them know that they will need to start looking around for a new place to live, I'm taking what's mine!'

Still, after everything is said and done, I still have my hypocrisies, I still have my doubts and my convictions. Everything that has culminated together throughout my short and universally insignificant little time that I call 'my excuse for life' is still here; it is still running at full speed and shows no signs of stopping anytime soon. Questions still rise up from the reptilian brain, logical damned things, practical in the most visceral and awing ways: "Who will get it right in the end? How will you be able to know when it ends? What will it feel like, emotionally, spiritually, physically, in every conscious manner of your being? What if there is nothing…then what? What if I'm wrong?"

"What if there is something there, and I was on the wrong side of the fence; how long can you claw for freedom before you eventually break?" Plagues of the mind, the spirit, the soul, the being; everything that you call 'yourself' depends upon how you structure your beliefs and reconciliations on matters of the ultimate question: "What is it all?"

For as long as I could remember, I had problems with the concept of faith, I just didn't get it…not really. I understood the stories and the songs, I even understood the little ceremonies that we had to go through on a regular basis. I just didn't understand why I didn't seem to act the same way about it as they did, or feel the same way, or talk the same way. I was a black sheep to the majority of the people that I was surrounded by for a rather substantial portion of my young life, though you would never know it at first glance. That was because I was fortunate enough to have been blessed with a 'family name' in the town that I spent the formidable years of my life in. Doesn't pull as much weight these days, a sign of the times I guess.

My fear was one of confusion, brought on by the cryptic and disturbingly twisted visions that were thrown into my dreams nightly (or damn near to it), for fourteen years! At no point in that span of time was I given any release from it. Every night, or as I stated before 'damn near to it', probably closer toward the 3–5 nights a week average, approximated of course; these days I'm lucky if I can remember my own name, if I'm asked in a hurry and I'm not quite paying attention, I'll panic.

Over and over and over…repeating itself with the same raw essence in every reprise as it had done in the first. Each time I would find myself feeling as if I were conscious, fully aware of everything that was going on around me, as if I wasn't even dreaming at all. It felt more real to me than the most surreal day that I have ever experienced in my life. Fourteen years of this never-ending story of violence, and at no time giving me any clues as to what the fuck was going on! Only questions, plenty of questions, I have more questions than I'm confident there are answers to at this point.

By now you are probably sitting there, leaning... tilting... drooling over what it could possibly be that could drive such a normal and centered child into this manner of frenzy. I believed in angels, and demons, and good, and evil, and heaven, and hell. Until I was left with more questions than answers, as we just covered. The scenery would change through a varied rotation of regular locations: caverns, mountains, valley plains that stretched for what looked like an eternity, and for all I knew...it did. The sky, when it could be seen, was like as if it had been torched; the clouds seemed to be lit with flames circling them, whispering in the wind. The atmosphere had changed to something unreal, filling your very core with emotions and ethereal states of being that cannot be quantified into words, all at once.

A flurry whips up in a dust devil that proceeds to carve its own little path through the chaos unfolding before me; it draws my eyes every time, slowly at first, then faster in wonder and curiosity, until finally the grand scope of what I am about to face yet again is presented before me. It is a slaughter; nothing else in my vocabulary can describe it any better. For endless miles upon miles, corpses can be found strewn across the landscape, some impaled within the forest of bodies that stretched as far as the eye can see, others just thrown around and laying as they fell.

It isn't the sights before me that give me the actual pain part of this experience, that is merely a demonstration of things to come. The pain is in the noise: it is a strange mixture of sounds, at one end of the spectrum there are the screams and wailings of these poor bastards that rush toward you like the sound of a river becoming a rapid, one ripple after another endlessly. The far side of the spectrum is the bizarre part because whereas before there was the chaos, now there is only silence, pure and perfect silence. It is the calmest, quietest silence I have ever known, nothing penetrated it; no sound, no vibration, no thought…emptiness. Both ends of this twisted spectrum of violence and puzzlement would meet together in my mind, not in my head…in my mind. I could hear everything but without using my ears, I could sense everything that was going on around me, yet I had no concept of distance from the sound, every effect that came to me sounded both far away and uncomfortably close and personal.

The screams blended with the silence in a way that I can only describe as this: Channel 1 has you focusing 100% of your listening to the screams, and wind, and atmosphere around you, while channel 2 has perfect silence, in which you lose every inch of yourself inside of it, no time, no state of…just perfect oblivion. Now, imagine if you were able to not only watch, but also dedicate the entirety of your faculties at focusing on each channel, but now put channel 1 and channel 2 on the same station. The best description that I can conjure up to describe what the effect of that is like is: 'A Harmonious Chaos'.

You may be wondering about the bodies: Who were they? What happened? Here are those answers as best as I can describe them…they were, I don't know…angels I guess. So many words flood into my thoughts when I think about that sight: horrific, brutal, epic, unreal, moving…all entwined at once and directed through my very core. I could feel them, their pain, their agony. I don't know how to describe it other than that I would shift my gaze from body to body, some dead, some dying; but all of those that still had breath in their lungs made it known. Each face brought with it a tidal wave of emotions that surged throughout my body, yet wouldn't let me express them, keeping everything inside with no physical reaction or stimuli…only the feeling.

Imagine the most painful crying fit that you have ever known, the pain that you feel from it, not a physical one (other than exhaustion and soreness), but rather one that tears straight through your very being. How hard it was, how tormented it sounded, and how broken you felt after. And imagine now that you could not release it, could not express it, you could not verbalize it or raise your voice to shake the very heavens, you could not release the pressure of the pain that builds within your spirit, coursing through your veins urging you, begging you to release it. But you can't, in the end there is nothing.

Every emotion, feeling, vibe, aura…whatever you choose to call it, that I have encountered within my lifetime, I saw and felt there upon that plain. I can still remember the feeling of discovering new ones that I have still yet to figure out how to even begin to classify them into rational and understandably explainable terms. All around me, I could feel it, no matter where I turned, no matter where I fixed my gaze…it was there. 'Please stop…please, make it stop.' I'm awake now…confused…short breath…sweaty…hands will stop shaking in a minute. It'll all be over soon…until tomorrow.

What a sad existence for those kind and downtrodden people. Just because you are insane doesn't mean that you should have to live in a torturous squalor with only your rants to keep you company. And what of those doctors and nurses? What kind of people are those that they can let the people, people who obviously need serious help and aren't receiving it where they are now, tire and suffer in the madness of their own distorted and abnormal minds? If they were truly kind and helpful medical professionals, they would just end it all for them…

"What?"

…put an end to their pain and their torment.

"How would that be better? To kill them? They may not have much of a life, but they at least have a life. And some of them are in there for good reasons; some are deaf, dumb and blind to their own senses, and others are deranged people who have killed and mutilated people! I would say that they are in as good a place as any for someone like themselves."

A life in a rotting shell of a former person, is no existence that anyone should have to endure. To be forced to look at yourself day after day and not know who or what you are? To be unable to communicate effectively with someone else, or to ever find someone who can see the world through your eyes, and express the same understanding and joy and love and wonder as you do. As far as I am concerned, that is an existence worse than death itself.

"As far as you're concerned...you're enjoying this. You're the one who keeps showing me these things, you're the one doing this, not me. So, don't try to make yourself sound so distraught and concerned over their well-being."

The graveyard was calm and still, quiet as the dead, except for one lone figure. Perched upon a gargoyle overlooking a mausoleum, the creature sat motionless, as if it were made from the very same marble that it sat upon. The shadows cascading from the trees in the moonlight seemed to flicker like a haunting beacon, casting its form upon all that it touched. All but that quiet figure. For hours it barely even stirred, until finally without a word it stood and fixed its gaze upon the tombstones.

The man could do nothing but to stand there and look upon it. The mausoleum itself was a modest and classical building, yet with an intimidating edifice. The shadows never seemed to stay in one place once cast, and the presence that this collection of marble and stone gave off, was one of old death and deep feelings. This was a place that had stood for a long time, and whatever was encased within its walls, was darker than anything that had been witnessed there that night. It was a truly ominous and evil looking place.

As he stood there and looked at this simple and great building, his gaze turned to the roof, upon a cross of stone, a grotesque was perched upon it. And something perched upon that. He could not see what it was that he now saw was sitting atop the gargoyle that watched over the mausoleum. Was it shadow or shape? Did he see it move, or was it merely a trickery of light and atmosphere?

"Do you now wish to see? Are you now ready?"

He could hear the voice coming from atop the gargoyle, emerging from some shadowy figure perched like a raven upon its master's shoulder. He could see its face, though it had no face to speak of, enveloped in the same nighttime darkness that surrounded it now. But he could see it. He could not see its mouth move, but he could hear it, and he knew it was coming from the creature.

"Ready for what?"

"Are you ready now? To see?"

He paused for a brief moment, tense and searching for any sense of calm or ease about the decision placed before him: 'Do I say no, and risk being tormented like this for more days, years, or forever? Or do I dare to say yes, and find myself hurled into something that I now know I am ill-equipped to see through to the end?'

His options fluttered throughout his mind as he began to calmly walk toward the great marble doors of the mausoleum, contemplating on what it was that he would find in there. What demonic thing will he witness this time? As the doors parted for him, he found himself standing in front of a marble sarcophagus. There was no name to be found anywhere on the stone, no marker as to who it was that was now encased before him. That is when he heard a voice coming from out of the tomb.

"An Unwanted Roommate"

I have known for a while now that I am not living in this house alone, and I use the term 'living' loosely. For the longest time I thought that maybe it was a small girl, it was curious about me, but not 'prankish' like little boys are. But now I am not so sure, I don't even know, no…I know that it isn't a child. It has always been curious, yes…but this is different. So far, it hasn't done anything malicious to me, but I am starting to get a serious concern for my safety.

Most of the time it is harmless, blowing puffs of air into my ear, whispering growls or whatever that sound is that it makes when I upset it. I've learned most of its rules by now: no open doors, no walking around upstairs between 3 a.m. and 3:30 a.m., no music in the bathrooms, and it hates it when you look directly at it. Most of the time it'll run away, and I won't even know that it's around for a few hours at least, but if it decides to stay…you should look away.

There are no eyes, not even a face to be honest, just the silhouette of it…but when you look at it you can feel it looking back at you. First, it growls almost as a cat does, that guttural type of growl, as if it was guarding its territory or felt defensive. I have not been brave enough to see how it would react if I stayed there, locked together in a stare. As I said, so far it hasn't done anything physically threatening, but I won't lie about it…this thing scares me. Now I fear that it is beginning to become bolder. Earlier today, while I was in the shower, it caressed the back of my leg. I know that it wasn't the water because: water flows down…this 'brushed' up, and I could feel a slight pressure behind it. It startled me so bad that I jumped out of reflex, not thinking about having a solid footing in the shower. I damn near slipped my way into a hospital emergency room. It shook me up so bad that I ended my shower right then and there… I never even made it to the conditioner.

"Something Wicked This Way Comes…"

It looks like…a little girl. At least what I prefer to think of as a little girl. Probably to keep the idea at bay and ease my fear that it may be malicious. It follows me around, watching me, stalking (but without the attack, just the observation), then nothing. I have tried to see it directly, when it peers around the stairway banister to see into the living room, acting like a child trying to watch the late-night movie over its parent's shoulders when it should be in bed. Glimpses are all that I see, blurs of motion swiftly followed by the softest sounds of heavy beats trailing up the stairway to the upper floor, before going silent again. It doesn't seem to be malicious or violent in any way, it acts with curiosity more than anything else. However, if it is a small child, my own little cherubim to watch over me, then there is still the remaining explanation needed for what has been watching me sleep at night.

This feels different, not like asking mommy to look for monsters in the closet before she leaves the door cracked for you, this is a real feeling of terror and panic. The most uncomfortable feeling of helplessness, nothing else exists but you...and it. I can't open my eyes...I don't want to open my eyes. I don't want to know what it is, what it looks like, where it is or what it is doing. I just want it to stop. I can feel it watch me, sometimes from behind, sometimes over me, and sometimes with me, in the bed. I wake up, like being jerked from a dream when someone yells, "Wake up, rise and shine, sleepy head!" (or some other tragic cliché phrasing that they decided to pull from their handbag of 'Random Terms and Phrases' that they've been filling since high school...before returning their tome of words to their pocket).

Just lying there now, I'm awake but I don't open my eyes, I don't move; I give no indication that I am conscious at all. But it knows, I don't know how but it does. I can feel it when it's near, topping off a paralyzing concoction of emotions, feelings, 'vibes'...whatever you what to call it. Imagine if you found yourself having a conversation with a person, you know where they are, you can see them, you can feel if they're uncomfortable, or lost, or happy. Nothing that you have ever been taught can explain to you why it is, or how it is that you can look at another person and just get a feeling inside of you (call it a gut intuition, a 'weird vibe', juju, etc...whatever) that tells you they are real and there. You just know it, you feel it, and you rationalize it and quantify it to the best of your abilities into something that makes sense to you and tells you when you're fine...and when you need to worry.

It just stands there, for minutes, 'til hours on end, moving only ever slightly either rising or enclosing. I cannot only feel it, but I can hear it. Not soft and sweet 'thuds' up a staircase, I can hear it breathing. It reminds me of almost a burning rubber smell, like 'smoking the tires' on a muscle car, but it wasn't that. It was subtler, not as distinct as that, but at the same time, it was also very pungent. It felt like it was soaking into the pores of my cheek and neck, like being in a humid environment, that moisture swirling through the currents of stagnant heat in the air. With every exhale there is a slight rumbling, not a growling (at least not one to stun or frighten with), more like an 'idling' sound. It wasn't trying to assert itself over me, it was like when you hear someone who has asthma or a wheeze in their chest when they breathe, just a steady repetition of rumblings and baffles.

I don't know why it chose me, what it wants, where it came from, or what to even do about it. I never move (as I said before), I never open my eyes, I hold myself back from coughing, or fighting with an itch. I keep having the terrible fear that if I were to open my eyes that it would be inches from my face, in whatever shape it has chosen to manifest itself into, staring right through me. No eyes…no eyes at all. But I can feel it, looking into the void of darkness that stands amidst the shadows of the night, eclipsing their natural blackness with its own, as if the very concept of the night had no meaning anymore. In full view before the blackest shadows that you could imagine attempting to peer into, majestically in all of its being and 'is', and its attention is wholly focused on me.

This has been the best way, so far that I have found, to describe the living hell that is my night. Only watching, nothing more, getting more curious, but always keeping a distance. This means that I can come to only two conclusions as to the events that have been taking place recently:

1. I have finally…after all my years of suffering with these feelings and emotionally paralyzing attacks…reached a state of mental stability that can only be described as, "Over the rainbow, I am crazy…"

2. It has either become suddenly curious about me…or it is just trying to mess with me for no obvious

reasoning that I can deduce, other than doing it 'just for the hell of it'.

Every night before I get into bed (just to throw a little personal information out there into the world), I always swipe my fingers between my toes; to clean out anything that might be in between them, lint, fuzz, whatever. It's kind of my 'thing', my ritual before bed, my own personal 'OCD' moment (which I have, just so you know. I am not trying to make a 'crass' joke or take a stab at disabilities...so there!). I'll take off my socks, then while still sitting on the side of the bed with my feet raised just enough for me to easily and effectively reach them, I'll clean in between my toes, wipe the bottom of my feet, then 'slide' myself into bed. Once my feet leave the ground, I don't put them back down (after all, what's the point in cleaning off the bottom of your feet if you're just going to put them back on something that could be dirty?).

I was lying in bed the other night, still quite awake and trying to relax my mind and ease it away from the torrent of petty problems that I decide to dedicate my daily efforts to worrying about. My feet were poking out from underneath the covers, not by much, but enough that you could tickle them if you wanted (which I think happens to be a very mean joke to pull on someone, especially when they aren't expecting it and have their guard down. It is hysterical; no questioning that part of it, but it's still mean). I have a hard time being able to become comfortable in a bed if my feet are covered up by the blankets...sheets too. I just cannot have anything on or over my feet when I'm trying to fall asleep. I don't know why, but from what I have been told by a few of my friends and close confidants, I'm not unique in that department.

Then, ever so gently, I felt it, a *swiping* sensation between my toes, just as I had done myself not fifteen minutes earlier. It wasn't air, no breeze from a fan, or slight gust from a cracked window or air conditioning unit turning on. This had a solid feeling to it, a physical presence with mass and movement. I thought that it was just an itch or a reflex the first time that it happened, so I scratched and rubbed them with my other toes, alternating my feet back in forth (sadly looking like a poor impersonation of a human attempting to be a cricket). Then that was the end of it, nothing else happened that night.

The calm can only last for so long before it is brushed aside by the storm. Four days, that has been my best record: Four days of nothing…just sleep and calm. It was simple at first, I still just figured that it was an itch (…'repeat step #1 as demonstrated earlier'), but then it became apparent to me that I was not only completely wrong in my assumptions, but that I was no longer alone. I can sit here now, typing this tale for all of you, and tell you that it felt like a real person was there, at the foot of my bed, 'playing' with my feet. There was nothing childish or innocent about this, this was like having to stay the night on the couch with 'that guy' in college (you know the kind that I'm talking about. The kind that always had to crack the towels at people in the shower, and who you never trusted with the keys).

I sat up completely freaked out and panicking trying to figure out what it was that had just happened to me. Then it hit me, that smell…that dull burning/chemical/rubber smell, and it is coming from in front of my bed. I can't see anything, no shape, no form, no mass, nothing. But I can smell it and I can feel it, motionless, vigilant, waiting as if to gauge my reaction and see what it is that I am going to do. Yet still, nothing. I lay my head back down, scrambling through the chaotic labyrinth that is my mind, searching for some hint or reference as to how I am supposed to process what just happened. Nothing.

I still do not know what it is, what it wants, or why it keeps doing what it does. I don't know what it looks like, or even where it is specifically at times. I can tell you that it has shown no decline in interest towards me, and has even begun to adventure out of its normal routines and show itself, if ever so briefly, running past from the stairs to the kitchen, then gone again. I think that I like the little girl better…she doesn't keep me up at night.

"Aces and Eights"

It has started to get worse, worse with the noises, but now there is more. Just a few nights ago, while I was sitting on my couch watching a movie, a bag of papers and random trash from spring-cleaning, which was sitting in corner of the kitchen, was knocked over and opened. As I heard the sound, I paused my movie, turned on the hallway light and made my way to the kitchen. There were no other sounds as I slowly crept to the switch on the kitchen wall. One flip of my finger later and I saw something that I have never before had happen...the trash bag had been untied and knocked over, after being placed in the center of the kitchen floor.

For that one brief moment, I felt my heart skip a beat, my lungs exhaled all that they had stored and refused to breathe, my legs went limp...only to regain their composure as if reacting out of reflex. It was like being weightless and removed from myself for that one split-second, something like the feeling you get in your stomach when you are on a rollercoaster, just after taking a plunge. I don't wish to feel that way again anytime soon, but I fear that was only the beginning, and that I am in for a lot more mischief and disorder in my world and my home, as time goes on. Since that night, I have begun to hear strange sounds at night, a heavy walking along the upstairs hallway between the two bedrooms, dishes moving and clanking against each other...I can hear talking in the bedroom above my living room. On more than one occasion, I would slowly make my way to the base of my stairs, preparing to ascend it, in order to investigate the source of these voices.

And on more than one occasion, I have been denied access by something at my stairs. It has growled at me, hissed at me, and when it *has* shown itself, it let no light past it; it was as if it had become this great wall placed upon the center of my staircase. It was brooding, and gave me a very unwelcome feeling, just before grumbling out its guttural warning, and forcing me back down the stairs with very little hesitation. I don't know what it is that I am supposed to do anymore. I feel like I am a prisoner in my own home; I am given numerous liberties to come and go as I please, to eat my fill and entertain myself as I wish…but if I happen to step out of line, even the slightest bit, it is quick to show me its disapproval. I have learned over the past two years of living here, that there are at least two entities living in my home with me, and while one is rather playful and curious, the other is far stricter and sharp with discipline.

Since learning that fact, I have now almost made it a habit to excuse myself if I happen to burp…in my own home, while by myself. Because if I do not show my manners and excuse myself, it lets me know that it does not approve of my actions, and it has done so in numerous ways. It has hissed into my ear just moments after, and it sounded as if there were a wildcat right beside me. I could feel the heat of breath on my ear and neck, and I could hear it as clear as the real thing, had it been there.

"King of the Mountain"

I have a nice enough home, it's not much, and far from what I have become accustomed to…but it's mine. It is a two-story condo, simple enough as they go, but it has all that I need. There is a small kitchen with a window that faces to the west, so that every time that you are cooking supper, and happen to be cooking it at just that right time, the kitchen would flood in with a cascade of colors from the sunset out on the horizon, past the forest and rooftops. There is a modest sized living room, more than capable of comfortably entertaining six people during a small dinner party, also partly in thanks to the fact that I was lucky enough to have a dining room as well. I have a bathroom across from my kitchen, and two decent bedrooms upstairs…but I don't use them anymore.

The 'master' bedroom has become nothing more than an oversized and glorified closet for my pantheon of wardrobes; I do not even have a bed in there. I have no need for one, since I sleep downstairs on the couch. I keep a mattress and a spare set of sheets in the second bedroom, just in case I happen to have any guests that wish to stay the night, but aside from that, I avoid going upstairs at all costs. I don't like it up there. It is not a creepy place in the sense that it is scary or anything, it has more to do with what is living there.

For some time now, I have been experiencing strange things, things that I cannot even begin to describe how they are even possible; I have been caressed and 'poked' while taking a shower, I have heard enormous 'bangs' against the walls every time that I play music. Even now as I write this to you, I have had two separate 'growls' directed at me…because I am writing about it. I know the growls; I know its sounds by now, deep, guttural, sharp. You know, the first time that I heard it…I honestly believed that somehow an angry dog had found its way into my house. It felt as if it were taking me *years* to get the courage up to turn around and see what had made that noise, half-expecting to see a Doberman poised right at me…waiting.

It only took me a fraction of a second as I spun around, more out of fear and bewilderment than anything else, only to find…nothing. Nothing else stood in that hallway with me, and as I stood staring at the bedroom door in front of me, I began to wonder if it may have just been the sound of a dog outside? Well, dear friends, if it had been that simple…then there would be no point in my telling this tale for you, would there? No, as I soon came to discover, whatever it was that had made those sounds at me, had found a new home…and was making itself comfortable.

I sleep on the couch because I do not like going up the stairs or near the stairs even. It likes to hang around there, peering around the banisters to see into the living room. Not everybody that comes through ends up seeing it, in fact most of them don't, which I am thankful for. Because for those who *do* see him, from that point on: <u>You</u> see him, and <u>he</u> sees you. Once that happens, so do the long nights and strange noises. If it knows that you can see it, and there is something about you that it happens to *not* like, then it will be sure to let you know.

The last time passing by on the stairs, as I moved past it, I could feel a sudden gust of desert scorching air blast into my face, swiftly followed by a sound that bellowed out at me that

I could only liken to a tiger when it is in a corner, attempting to swat off another animal. Fast, sharp, deep, rumbling.

The 'growl', that I have now become somewhat accustomed to over our time together, caught me so off guard that I nearly found myself falling backwards down the steps to the hardwood planks below. Saved only by sheer reflex, reaching out for the banister railings, all the while attempting to wrap my brain around what had just happened to me.

Nearly a week ago, it managed to do some real injury to me, as it proceeded to push me down an entire flight of stairs. From the little that I remember of the incident, as I was at the top of the stairs preparing to descend, I remember feeling two hands press up against my back...and push. Then down the stairs I went, tumbling head over feet, bouncing between the wall and the stair railing, as I made my chaotic and painful way to the base of the steps, where I had a small metal toolbox sitting. As I reached the bottom of the stairs, my head hit the toolbox, briefly knocking me unconscious. I awoke nearly an hour later with a splitting headache and a lot of questions as to what just happened to me.

Over the time that it has lived with me, while it may touch me from time to time, it has never done anything malicious. This new event terrified me, and became the final factor in deciding to remain downstairs, effectively abandoning the entire second floor of my home. I shouldn't have to give up my home, my bed, my shower, my bathroom...but whatever it is that has now decided to make my second floor its home, it has definitely made its intentions known. I have very real fears beginning to form within me, and I am beginning to have very real doubts as to whether or not I may even survive the next encounter.

"The Boogeyman Is Real..."

What do you do when you know that the Boogeyman exists, and you can't get away from him? For years lying dormant, drifting off into the deep reaches of mere memory that never resurfaces on their own. Laying quietly, watching, stalking, and preparing for his next 'visit'. People grow, adapt, evolve, mature, and begin to no longer fear certain things that they once did, when the closet wasn't shut completely.

So, it watches from a distance, never straying too far from reach. It studies me, seeing what it is that terrifies me now; now that I know of true horror, true despair, what unchecked violence can do to the world and those unfortunate enough to be caught up in it. So much more horror than we ever knew existed, or could exist in the world. So much more to fear. I can't live like this anymore. The next opportunity that I get to try and kill that specter once and for all, I'm taking it.

"The final police records would eventually state, that in a fit of psychotic rage, you were disarmed and detained."

"Me? Detained? What do you mean me?"

"A neighbor of yours had called the police about strange and violent sounds coming from your home. So naturally the police came by and looked, trying to find out if everything was alright and everyone inside was safe."

"What are you talking about?"

"But when the police had finally arrived, all that they found was you, fighting with yourself, cutting and gauging out chunks of flesh from your own arms. Fighting frantically, wrestling with only yourself."

"This is insane…"

"Yes, it is."

The stranger looked up from his tomb to lock eyes with the same creature he had spoken to throughout the night, the same that he had seen move in the shadows, and had once been perched above the very building they both now stood inside of.

"But how? Why?"

"Why? Why you were 'seeing' things that were not there? Why you chose to attack yourself? Or perhaps 'why did I kill them'?"

"Kill them? Kill who? I've never…"

"Your live-in girlfriend of six years and her four-year-old daughter…"

"Daughter…"

The stranger tried to rack his brains for some acknowledgment of these statements. He became pained, panicked, and frantic as he felt the entire life and history of what he had done flood into his core. Every feeling, every emotion, every moment that he took in the middle of the night, to tie up his girlfriend and her daughter to the master bed. The lucid and awesome sights that became branded into his memory, and the reflection of the aftermath of his carnage, always reeking in his mind of stale rust and copper.

"My god, I did it."

"...butchered by a man who in turn would try to butcher himself as well. Butchered by a man who would leave their lifeless and destroyed corpses in his bed, to wreak, rot, and sour, as he quietly slipped away into the abyss of his mind."

The stranger looked at the creature in front of him. As he locked eyes with it, he could finally see his final moment.

Judgment Day

"At the directive of the Ninth District Courthouse, for the crimes of murder, and mutilation of a corpse, for the defilement of the dead, and the deadly assault of two county sheriff's deputies, this execution is to be carried out immediately and on this day, the third of July. Before this execution is to take place, do you have any final statement?"

I always did hate the feeling of cold metal on my skin. The chair was painful in its construction alone, but then again, I don't think that they had comfort in mind when they designed it. The most embarrassing moment outside of when they shave off all your hair, is when they fit you with an adult diaper...just in case you happen to relieve yourself as you're on your way out. This was by far not one of my finest hours, I am certain of that.

"I just want everybody to know, that I still wish I could take it all back. But I can't take back what I did. I know that I wasn't myself, but that doesn't excuse what I did. I just want to say that it sucks when shit happens, and this sucks."

What else was I going to say to them? 'Sorry about killing your daughter and granddaughter?' 'Sorry about cutting them up?' They got two years of news stories and gossip out of all of that already, why keep pandering to the crowd and feeding the wolves at their heels? They made up their minds, and they decided to kill me. And as best as I can tell, there is nothing that I can do about that fact now. There's nothing that I would care to contribute to it, but sadly nothing that I can do to prevent it either. Now it's only me, only me and old sparky, about to ride the lightning.

"So, let's get this over with, shall we?"

After all, if there's nothing that you can do about a situation that is about to unfold before you, regardless of what actions you may take to try and prevent it, why stand on ceremony? You might as well just get on with it and get it all over with. None of us wanted to be here all day.

"Very well. Executioner, do your duty."

There was a brief moment of darkness as the lights switched over to the generator. And by the time that they had risen back up, the man that was before them, braced and ready for his death, was now locked, tense, and shaking violently. The electricity coursed so violently throughout his body, that as he sat there, convulsing, the sound of his spine could be heard snapping over the sound of the turbines that powered this morbid spectacle. His head began to rattle as it fought the urge to shoot off of his body with all of the force and passion of a fourth of July fireworks display.

I can feel the cold wash over me, wrapping itself around my body from head to toe. It comes from nowhere, suddenly chilling, feeling as though the seasons had changed to the dead of winter, with no shelter to hide you. It comes before the change, a sort of indicator of things to come. The air changes, taking on a new bizarre bouquet of stale death, that stagnant smell that you get around the swamps...heavy, damp. Even the pressure around you will begin to pop your ears, force against your sinuses, and make you feel as though you're under eight feet of water. Then a still calm, numbness in everything, perfect silence. Then, as quickly as it had arrived and engulfed me, it was gone. It was over.

The sarcophagus gently slid open. The stranger stared down into the hollow chamber that had been decorated and laid out for him.

"Are you ready?"

The stranger looked up at the creature, before taking one last breath. Slowly but purposefully, he crawled into the tomb, laying down and resting his head upon the velvet pillow placed inside. As the lid closed, he could see the creature lift its head and stare toward the mausoleum doors, its attention drawn by some new and great spectacle outside in the cemetery... The creature swiftly made its way out of the doors, just as it heard the stone lid of the tomb inside grind and slam, as it sealed itself shut. And as the mausoleum doors closed, the creature's gaze became locked and focused on a strange sound coming from the distance. There it sat, and watched the entrance to the graveyard, perched back upon its cross of marble and stone.

It could hear the voice, but it wasn't sure, which direction it was coming from, or how far away it might be. That is when the creature froze upon the stone grotesque atop the mausoleum, and began to watch and stalk, as the voice came closer and pierced through the darkness:

"Hello? Is there anybody out there?"

The End

www.ingramcontent.com/pod-product-compliance
Lightning Source LLC
Chambersburg PA
CBHW070536130626
46555CB00003B/1441